Angel swallowed. "I'll never forget... this." And you.

An ache was spreading in her chest as it hit her what and whom she would be leaving behind when she left. The place that had been home to her for a part of practically every summer since she was a kid. Home and a place of magic, with fairy hills and fiddles, and lifetime friends like Bernadette. *And the promise of something more with Gabe.*

Was it some stellar force that was drawing her closer to him? Making her want to kiss him again? Ignoring all the warning bells in her head, she closed the short distance between them and had barely murmured her thanks when his hands shifted to draw her into his embrace. Their cheeks brushed against each other briefly and she heard Gabe draw in his breath before their lips met.

Angel threw caution to the wind and returned his kiss readily, pressing her hands against his broad back.

Dear Reader,

Who hasn't experienced a time when their trust was broken, or when their heart was broken by a loss, romantic or not?

My heroine Evangeline ("Angel") travels to scenic Cape Breton Island to settle her grandmother's affairs, sell "Gramsy's" B and B, and return to her home and teaching job in Toronto. She doesn't expect her past feelings for Gramsy's neighbor Gabriel, sparked during her summer visits and whom she hasn't seen for ten years, to be reignited. Now a Michelin-starred executive chef, Gabe has relocated permanently to the island from Scotland and opened a second restaurant.

Angel and Gabe felt the chemistry between them in the past, but their lives were an ocean apart, and their connection faded as they pursued their careers. Their mutual love for Gramsy and the terms of her will open the door to new possibilities. But the arrival of Gabe's ex-fiancée complicates matters, and Angel's trust of Gabe is shattered, compounded by her bitter experience with her past boyfriend.

I was inspired to write their love story after a trip to the iconic Canadian island. Won't you return there with me and experience the magic of Angel and Gabriel's reunion?

Love,

Rosanna xo

REUNITED WITH THE TYCOON NEXT DOOR

ROSANNA BATTIGELLI

H Harlequin
ROMANCE

If you purchased this book without a cover you should be aware that this book is stolen property. It was reported as "unsold and destroyed" to the publisher, and neither the author nor the publisher has received any payment for this "stripped book."

Harlequin® ROMANCE

ISBN-13: 978-1-335-47051-5

Reunited with the Tycoon Next Door

Copyright © 2025 by Rosanna Battigelli

All rights reserved. No part of this book may be used or reproduced in any manner whatsoever without written permission.

Without limiting the author's and publisher's exclusive rights, any unauthorized use of this publication to train generative artificial intelligence (AI) technologies is expressly prohibited.

This is a work of fiction. Names, characters, places and incidents are either the product of the author's imagination or are used fictitiously. Any resemblance to actual persons, living or dead, businesses, companies, events or locales is entirely coincidental.

For questions and comments about the quality of this book, please contact us at CustomerService@Harlequin.com.

TM and ® are trademarks of Harlequin Enterprises ULC.

Harlequin Enterprises ULC
22 Adelaide St. West, 41st Floor
Toronto, Ontario M5H 4E3, Canada
www.Harlequin.com

Printed in U.S.A.

Recycling programs for this product may not exist in your area.

Rosanna Battigelli loved Harlequin Romance novels as a teenager and dreamed of being a romance writer. For a family trip to Italy when she was fifteen, she packed enough "Harlequins" to last the month! Rosanna's passion for reading and love of children resulted in a stellar teaching career with four Best Practice Awards. And she also pursued another passion—writing—and has been published in over a dozen anthologies. Since retiring, her dream of being a Harlequin Romance writer has come true!

Books by Rosanna Battigelli

Harlequin Romance

Swept Away by the Enigmatic Tycoon
Captivated by Her Italian Boss
Caribbean Escape with the Tycoon
Rescued by the Guarded Tycoon
Falling for the Sardinian Baron

Visit the Author Profile page at Harlequin.com.

To all the loved ones we have lost,
and the memories we will never lose.

Especially for Ma, Dad, Pina, Nelda, GG,
Grampsy from Nova Scotia, and our beloved Alain.

We love you, we miss you,
and you're always in our hearts.

Praise for Rosanna Battigelli

"I was hooked from the first page to the very last one.
I fell in love with the characters as I read. The chemistry
between them sets the pages alight as you read.
I can't wait to read more from this author in the future.
Highly recommended author."
—*Goodreads* on *Swept Away by the Enigmatic Tycoon*

CHAPTER ONE

A PASSENGER'S SNEEZE a few seats behind her startled Angel from her all-too-brief nap. She straightened in her seat and inhaled and exhaled deeply. She couldn't help shivering a little from the anticipation of reaching Halifax. The flight from Toronto wasn't an especially long one—three hours—but it had been delayed twice, set to arrive finally at 7:00 p.m. instead of early afternoon.

Angel had been looking forward to arriving at the Halifax airport early, picking up the rental car she had booked and proceeding leisurely up the scenic coast to her destination: a quaint B&B still another four hours away in the French Acadian fishing village of Chéticamp Island, off the northwest side of Cape Breton Island. Her Gramsy's B&B. Known by the same name.

A sharp prickle beneath her eyelids made her turn to the window to conceal any tears from the other passengers across the aisle, several of whom were also sitting up and checking their watches or phones. There was nobody in the two seats next to her, yet she was afraid to give in to her vulnerability in public. She bit her lip, refusing to let surface those unbridled emotions, even if they *were* silent tears.

Her grandmother's B&B was imprinted in her mind: a two-story lemon-yellow saltbox with sea-blue-and-white-striped canopies over the top-floor windows and front door. Red, coral and yellow begonias interspersed with purple trailing verbena and the startling yellow-green of potato vine spilled over each of the white window boxes.

The wide steps leading up to the front entrance welcomed guests with splashes of color from the flowers in each glazed ceramic pot on either side. Petunias of all shades, their bright blossoms encircled by a lacy foliage border of dusty miller. You couldn't help but catch your breath at the floral wonder that greeted you and led to the front door and roomy wraparound deck.

Whenever Angel had visited Gramsy in previous summers, she always paused at the entrance gate to take in the picture-perfect scene of the house set against a cloudless, baby blue Atlantic sky and the deeper hue of the Gulf of Saint Lawrence. Walking up to the double front door, she would inevitably catch the mouthwatering scent of one or more freshly baked pies: apple or blueberry, and most certainly, her favorite, wild berry pie. Moments later, she would be nestled in Gramsy's warm embrace, and promptly ushered into the farmhouse kitchen for a generous slice—or two—of steaming pie topped by a scoop of creamy vanilla ice cream.

Angel blinked to stem the wave of emotions evoked by the memories. *Sadness. Regret. Guilt.* All feelings that she knew would intensify once she was actually on Gramsy's doorstep. And in the days after, concentrating on what she would have to do.

Her thoughts dissipated at the pilot's announcement of their imminent landing. Yawning, Angel tucked her magazine into a compartment of her handbag and focused on the twinkling city lights as the plane descended.

Minutes later, she was at the rental car office with her suitcase, wondering why it was taking so long for the employee to call up her booking.

"I'm so sorry," the middle-aged man finally said with a shrug. "Your booking seems to have been canceled."

Angel blinked. "That's impossible. Why would I cancel it? In fact, I called your office last week to confirm my booking." She heard her voice rise an octave. "I need a car. *Now*." She turned as she sensed another person moving next to her.

"There's no need to panic," a deep voice announced. "I can explain."

A voice with a Scottish brogue. Angel looked up to connect the voice to the impossibly tall man next to her. Her head was level with his chest and as she craned her neck farther to meet his glance directly, a muscle pulled and she involuntarily raised her hand to her neck with a grimace. *Really?* she thought. *Now?*

She took a step back, trying to ignore the soft thudding of her heart, as her gaze locked with ocean eyes that had enchanted her in the past with alternating hues of teal and blue green. Enchanted her until the rose-colored glasses she had been wearing had finally faded when he decided not to return to the island ten years ago.

Gabe. Gabe McKellar, the owner of the estate next to Gramsy's property and B&B.

How had *he* managed to get her booking canceled? Just because he was a celebrated Michelin-starred chef who delighted Gramsy and the islanders with his permanent return, what made him think he could overstep like this? Why was he here in the first place?

Angel's stomach twisted. She was tired and emotional, and the last thing she expected was to not have a rental car at her disposal and to have

Gabe McKellar show up, declaring that he could explain why her booking had been canceled.

She glanced back at the employee with a frown. He shrugged and gestured for Gabe to continue.

"I was instructed to pick you up personally to take you to Chéticamp," he said calmly, looking at her unwaveringly as he stroked his groomed beard.

Angel felt her jaw drop. "By whom? And why?" She crossed her arms and stared up at him defiantly.

Gabe held her gaze without blinking. "By your Gramsy," he said, lowering his voice. "I'll explain further on our way to the B&B." He reached for her suitcase. "May I?"

His mention of Gramsy was the last thing Angel had expected to hear. Her heart began to hammer loudly and she bit her lip. "Look, Angel, I know it's been a long time since…since we—"

"Since you left the island," she said coolly.

"Actually, I was going to say it's been a long time since we chased each other around your Gramsy's apple trees." He grinned, showing perfect teeth.

Angel blinked. She had met Gabe over the many summers she had visited her maternal grandparents, "Gramsy" and "Grampsy," at their B&B in Chéticamp. He was their neighbor's grandson visiting from Scotland. She was seven when she had first met him, and Gabe ten, with a shock of curling black hair and a penchant for challenging her to a race, whether around the trees or along the sandy shore of their stretch of island. He had stopped coming to the island ten years ago, only to return permanently three years back. After ten years, here again was that black-haired boy—man now—smiling at her as if nothing had happened between them.

Nothing had happened between them.

Angel's jaw tightened. How could he even bring up the past at a time like this? Feeling her cheeks burn, she turned to the employee self-consciously, but to her relief, he was assisting another customer.

"I'm sorry," Gabe said gruffly. "Can we start over? It's been a long time and… I'm very sorry for the loss of your Gramsy," he said more softly. He started to extend his hand, then let it drop. "Welcome back to Nova Scotia, Angel."

Gabe was all too aware of Angel's brown eyes blurring when he expressed his condolences.

"Thank you," she said, and quickly turned away to dab at both eyes before facing him again.

"May I?" He reached again for her luggage and she nodded curtly before following him to the exit doors.

From the look of Angel's furrowed brows and pursed lips, she obviously had mixed feelings about the situation. She must be curious about *him* being designated to meet her at the airport and drive her back to the B&B, while also trying to process the recent passing of her grandmother, her *Gramsy*—who was known and beloved by most islanders, and who'd left a lasting impression on anyone fortunate enough to have booked and stayed at her B&B.

When Gabe reached his Range Rover, he opened the passenger door for Angel and when she was settled in, he proceeded to place her luggage in the trunk. She must not be planning to stay long on Chéticamp Island, he mused, if the weight of her suitcase had anything to do with it.

"You must be tired," he said, starting the ignition. "Look, Angel, why don't you just sit back, relax and even nod off if you want to. There's plenty of time tomorrow to meet and talk about your grandmother's wishes and—"

"Are you a lawyer, too?" she said bluntly.

Gabe glanced at her, his foot still on the brake. "No, I—"

"Well, then, I'll wait to talk to her lawyer, if that's okay."

Gabe caught the glint in her eyes before proceeding to exit the airport parking lot. A look that made it clear that he was treading on sensitive territory. That her grandmother's business was none of *his* business.

He nodded. "No problem. Are you hungry? Would you like me to stop for anything?"

"No thanks," she said gruffly. "Look, Gabe, I don't know why *you* were sent to pick me up, but after the almost seven-hour flight delay, I'm beat. I…didn't mean to be rude," she added more softly. "I just can't process anything more tonight." She yawned into her hands before adjusting her seat to a reclining position. Leaning back, she closed her eyes, her hands clasped in her lap.

Gabe gazed at Angel for a few seconds before concentrating on merging into the highway traffic, and once he was comfortably in his lane, he glanced over again at the granddaughter of the woman who had been like a grandma to him, too. In fact, he had also called her Gramsy. She had insisted on it.

His parents owned the property next to Gramsy's, a two-acre piece of prime land that was settled by the McKellars, his father's Scottish ancestors, centuries earlier. They were among the fifty thousand Highland Scots who settled on Cape Breton Island in the late eighteenth and early nineteenth century. Gabe's parents had business interests in Scotland, but they made sure to return yearly to what they considered to be one of the friendliest places on earth. Gabe was their only son, and bringing him to Nova Scotia and Cape Breton Island for a month every summer became a tradition that Gabe always looked forward to. He loved watching the waves of the Gulf of Saint Lawrence froth and darken in a storm, while he was safe inside the reinforced Tudor-style estate his grandfather had commissioned to be built in the 1950s.

Angel's yearly summer visit to Chéticamp had coincided with his visit up until ten years ago, when he was accepted at Le Cordon Bleu in France. He distinguished himself during his culinary training and was offered several apprentice and sous-chef opportunities afterward in Italy and Switzerland, resulting eventually with the opening of his own restaurant, Maeve's—named after his mother—in Edinburgh. His dedication and innovative dishes resulted in the granting of his first Michelin star, after which his success flourished and he no longer needed his parents' financial support. He only returned to Chéticamp after the tragic death of his parents in a car accident, needing time to process their passing as well as his recently broken engagement.

In the last three years since he moved permanently to Chéticamp, he had opened a second restaurant and gained another Michelin star. During that time, Angel hadn't visited at all.

Gabe glanced over at Angel. Her long lashes rested above cheekbones that were flushed. Her mouth was no longer pursed, and her rhythmic breathing confirmed his suspicions that she was sleeping. *It hadn't taken long.* He noticed her pulse in the curve of her neck, and something stirred in his chest. She looked so lovely, with her shoulder-length auburn hair framing her heart-shaped face.

She had blossomed into a beauty. Not that she was unattractive when she was young. At ten years of age, he had met her at a tea party at Gramsy's. A party Gramsy had planned specifically to try to get the seven-year-old Angel out of her shell. So, she had invited him along with his parents, as well as a girl named Bernadette, the granddaughter of her friends farther down the coast.

Gabe recalled noting the difference between Angel and Bernadette. Angel was shy, quiet and reserved, with pigtails or braids tightly in place, and wearing a brightly colored sundress, while Bernadette was a free spirit with long, strawberry blond hair and freckles, flitting about in T-shirt and shorts, doing pirouettes and cartwheels around the adults, and interrupting their conversation to add a lengthy and spirited story of her own. He liked them both, and by the middle of her vacation, Angel too was more relaxed and allowed herself to join in the races that he and Bernadette made a part of every encounter. A couple of times, when Bernadette couldn't join them, he and Angel had spent hours together, riding their bikes along the Chéticamp Island roads, their baskets loaded up with sandwiches and fruit for their inevitable picnic later on a huge, flat outcrop at one section of the beach, in full view of Gramsy's B&B.

They would eat silently, watching the waves rise up and cascade over the beach, the soft, swooshing sound mingling with the cries of the gulls overhead. Angel would stop eating and always made the comment that the foam spreading over the sand reminded her of the lacy hem of a wedding dress. The dress of a princess, she had added dreamily, before biting back into her sandwich. And afterward, she would pull one of her books—often a fairy tale—out of the basket behind her bike seat, and be completely absorbed for a while, leaving him to build sandcastles and delight in seeing a rogue wave knock it over and splash him in the process. She would join him in collecting unusual shells strewn along the coast, and sometimes they would trade one for the other's.

Ultimately, Gramsy would call out to them

from the back deck. A slice of pie and milk later, and Gabe would then run or ride back to his summerhouse.

For Angel's birthday on August 17—which always fell during both their visits—Gramsy would have a small birthday party for her, inviting Gabe and Bernadette. Gabe would bring a gift and include a special shell that he had found. On the inside, he would print his initial in permanent marker. He would always be pleased by Angel's delight over the shell, and it became a tradition to add to her shell collection on her birthday.

When she turned sweet sixteen, he gave her a heart-shaped shell he had found washed up on the beach after a storm a few days earlier. It was a delicate pink that reminded him of the flush in Angel's cheeks, especially when she was adamant about something. He brought it home, cleaned it and put it in a special box. It had a tiny hole and could be made into a pendant, but he was too shy to offer it to Angel like that. He presented it to her after a stroll on the beach rather than in front of everybody at her birthday dinner.

Gabe was surprised that these memories were resurfacing. *Again.* He wondered if Angel recalled such details. *Probably not.* Was she still a dreamer, perhaps wondering if one day *her* prince would sweep her away? He glanced over at her. She was missing the beauty of the splashes of gold and orange against the darkening sky. For a moment, her eyelids fluttered, and he wondered—*hoped*—that she would wake up and catch it before it dissipated. *And so they could talk.*

Instead, she inhaled deeply and shifted to the side closest the window, her hands intertwined. No ring on her left hand, he noted before turning his attention once again to the highway. It would be about four and a half hours before they reached Chéticamp Island. His drive to Halifax airport hadn't seemed that long, with a stop at his restaurant in Inverness and then a leisurely dinner at one of his favorite restaurants at the Halifax harbor before heading to the car rental place to pick up Angel.

He had canceled the car rental a couple of days earlier, when Gramsy's lawyer went over the instructions she had left specifically for him, written months earlier, but only to be revealed to Gabe shortly before Angel's arrival.

He took a deep breath and exhaled slowly. The week ahead was undoubtedly going to be a hard one for Angel, being her first return in three years, and having missed Gramsy's last days. *She's worked so hard as a teacher in Toronto these past ten years,* Gramsy had told Gabe during afternoon tea one day when he stopped in to check on her. *And taking special courses over the last three summers. She deserves a break.* She had gone on to wistfully tell Gabe that although she missed Angel's visits, they chatted and video called regularly.

A slight pattering against his windshield confirmed the earlier weather report. Steady rain throughout the night, with increasing winds and likely a series of thunderstorms, due to the tropical storms gathering momentum in the Gulf of Mexico and swirling their way up the Atlantic coast to the Maritime Provinces.

He stole another glance at Angel. She still had a sprinkling of light freckles on her face, and her lips were—

His head snapped back to the traffic. He could not let himself be distracted by the lips that had granted him his first kiss...

The intermittent flash of the approaching car's headlights alerted him that police were up ahead. He checked his speed and concentrated on staying within the safe speed limit instead of conjuring up memories that should remain buried.

The first part of the lengthy drive to Chéticamp and Gramsy's B&B was to get to the Canso Causeway that connected mainland Nova Scotia to Cape Breton Island. It would take two and a half hours from the airport to the causeway. After that was crossed, the road snaked along the western flank of the island to almost the northern tip. It was beautiful and scenic during the day in fine weather, but in inclement conditions, especially with reduced visibility at night and during a storm, it could get downright risky. Gabe was prepared to stop on the way if need be, and from the sudden pelting, it seemed more than likely that they would have to do so. He reduced his speed, surprised that Angel hadn't budged. Of course, she was exhausted from the ordeal of the long delay at the airport, and most likely from the anticipation of dealing with Gramsy's affairs once she arrived.

A flash of lights from a truck zooming closer and then passing him, sending an unwelcome spray against his window, made his heart jolt and he swerved. *Too close for comfort.* He clenched his jaw. "*Damn idiot!*" he muttered as he edged back in his lane, causing Angel to slide against his right shoulder. The motion did not wake her up, though, and he had no intention of trying to do so.

Her proximity unsettled him. With her breath fanning his arm and the lilac scent of her perfume wafting up to him, it felt as if she were a girlfriend he was bringing home after a date.

The guy racing by had unsettled him, too, as he could have ended up skidding off the road to prevent a collision with the truck, endangering his life and Angel's.

Fortunately, by the time they arrived at the causeway, the rain had subsided, and Gabe continued north to Highway 19, which would snake its way parallel to the coastal waters of the gulf and turnoff at Chéticamp Island Road, a road along a sandbar that led to Chéticamp Island. With any luck, they would arrive at Gramsy's B&B before the predicted thunderstorm.

He had picked up a few groceries earlier and left them in the fridge and on the counter for Angel. Being Gramsy's closest neighbor, he had often looked in on her to see if she needed anything, and she had found it more convenient to entrust him with a key in case she lost hers or was upstairs, having a nap. Two months ago, when he was returning with Gramsy's mail at her request, he entered to find her pale and gasping for air at her kitchen counter.

Knowing it would take much longer to wait for the paramedics to arrive, he helped her into his Range Rover and drove to the emergency department at the Chéticamp Community Health Centre. She underwent a series of tests, which confirmed that she had suffered a small stroke. A month later, having accepted her invitation for tea, he walked over with a bouquet of wildflowers from his own garden, only to find her napping on her swing that looked out over the bluff to the beach.

His heart had stopped when he realized she wasn't napping. He called the paramedics immediately. After the vehicle sped away, he sat down on the swing and let the tears flow at the loss of the dear woman who had always treated him like a grandson.

The memories of that day made his eyelids prickle. He blinked rapidly, needing his vision to stay clear. At that moment, Angel woke up and gazed up at him, and realizing she was nestled against him, quickly jerked away and sat upright.

"Sorry about that," she murmured with an embarrassed laugh. "You should have shaken me off." She checked the time on her phone and groaned. "Still two hours away." Peering at the winding road ahead, she said, "Any chance of stopping for a coffee and a sandwich? I'm feeling hungry now. All I had on the plane was a bag of roasted almonds and water."

Gabe nodded, relieved to shelve his memories. "A gas station and diner are coming up soon. Can you survive till then?"

The corners of her mouth lifted. "I guess so. Just warning you, though. Don't be alarmed at the sound of my stomach grumbling. It usually frightens small children and animals."

Gabe couldn't help laughing. "I'm neither a child nor an animal, so I should be fine."

"Well, I warned you," she murmured, averting her gaze.

CHAPTER TWO

Fifteen minutes later, Gabe pulled into the mostly empty parking lot of an all-night diner. The Cabot Trail Diner, open only a year, Gabe mentioned, but always busy during the day and evenings. Angel looked around, liking the retro vibe with its booths on the periphery of the room, and round pedestal tables arranged around the center, their padded chair seats and backs a variety of '50s-style colors: red, mint, teal, coral and yellow.

Gabe chose a booth, and to Angel's dismay, her stomach grumbled loudly as she surveyed the menu. Gabe pretended to jump back in his seat. She felt her cheeks flushing, and she looked around self-consciously.

"You were right," he said teasingly. "It's a good thing that there are no children on the premises at this hour."

Angel didn't reply. The flash of his eyes and smile were disconcerting in the bright light of the diner. He was no longer the cute, twenty-three-year-old guy next door to Gramsy. With his straight nose, strong jaw and closely shaven mustache and beard—and perfect lips—Gabe had become drop-dead gorgeous. In the ten years since Angel had seen him, the lanky frame of his youth and young adulthood had changed to a physique that only dedicated workouts could produce, she mused, as he took off his all-weather jacket and rolled up his shirtsleeves, revealing his sculpted arm muscles and broad chest and shoulders. A small patch of curly hair peeked out of the open V of his shirt, and sensing his eyes on her, Angel averted her gaze quickly and focused on her menu.

When the waitress came over and greeted them, accusing Gabe of "being a stranger," he apologized with a chuckle. "Meet my friend Angel," he said. "Angel, Heather."

Heather grinned and took their order. A turkey and brie on rye for her, and a chicken clubhouse for Gabe. "Wanna split an order of fries?" he said. "They pile them on."

"Um, sure." Angel said, glancing from him to Heather, who she was sure was gazing at her with curiosity. "Oh, and a coffee, please, with milk."

"Ditto," Gabe said. "But black for me. I need to stay awake for the rest of the way."

Heather's eyebrows arched at Gabe, but she didn't comment. "It won't be long," she said, taking their menus and walking away.

Angel looked past Gabe to the framed posters on the wall, featuring the stars of the '50s: Lucille Ball, Doris Day, Rock Hudson, Elvis and more. She was too embarrassed to look at Gabe directly. He had introduced her as his *friend*, even though they hadn't seen each other for ten years. Yes, they had been childhood friends for a few weeks over two decades' worth of summers, but how could he still consider her a friend? From the way the waitress had glanced from Gabe to her, she must have wondered if they were more than just friends… Angel excused herself to go to the ladies' room. Hopefully it wouldn't be long before their food was ready. A wave of fatigue washed over her. And sadness over the reason for her trip. She just wanted to get to Gramsy's and curl up in the four-poster bed in the spare bedroom Gramsy kept for her and her alone. The three other bedrooms were designated for the B&B guests.

She couldn't wait to get there. And spill the tears that had been building up during the flight. She looked at herself in the mirror. Hair a little skewed, eyeliner blurred, shadows under her eyes. Cheeks still flushed. She ran a comb through her hair, wiped away the smudges and, taking a deep breath, returned to their table, which already held two steaming cups of coffee.

"Good timing," Gabe said, as Heather approached with their orders. She set the bowl of fries between them.

"Now, don't fight over them." She grinned. "There's plenty for both of you." She met Gabe's gaze. "Ketchup and vinegar are coming," she chuckled. "Enjoy."

Angel was glad that there was minimal talk between them as they dug into their sandwiches. Gabe gave a thumbs-up after taking a few bites and Angel nodded. He squirted a corner of his side of the fries with ketchup and vinegar. Angel did the same with only the ketchup. When they bumped fingers as they reached for a fry, their gazes met. "After you, Angel," he said. "Just leave me one or two."

Was he always such a teaser? Yes, he *had* teased her when they were kids. Gentle teasing, not mean. At first, she had been too shy to give it back to him, but as she got older, she'd sometimes initiate and he would just laugh. "Okay," she said brightly, and impulsively pulled his entire bowl toward her. "Will do." She deliberately dipped one of her fries in his pool of ketchup and then plopped it in her mouth, while staring at him boldly.

He let out a deep laugh that drew the attention of the other customers. Heather sauntered over. "Wow, Angel. You must be pretty special for Gabe to turn over all his fries to you," she chuckled. "He's pretty proprietorial about them."

Angel shrugged. "He said for me to just leave him one or two," she replied innocently, before choosing one of his longest fries and plopping one end into her mouth. Heather and Gabe laughed and Heather shot Gabe a knowing look before walking away to greet new customers.

"Just kidding," Angel murmured, sliding the bowl back in the middle. "Go crazy. I'm full."

"I appreciate your generosity," he said. "I'm *not* full."

Angel sipped her coffee as Gabe finished the rest of the fries. Despite her protests a few minutes later, Gabe insisted on taking the bill. "My pleasure," he said when she thanked him with a sigh of resignation. "Happy to keep your growling at bay."

Heather thanked Gabe for his generous tip and they rushed back into the Range Rover, the returning rain starting to gain momentum. In the car, Angel kept her eyes on the road ahead. There were many dark and narrow stretches, and she didn't want to distract Gabe. Even when bushes appeared on either side of the road, Angel was all too aware that to the west of them was the steady companionship of the Gulf of Saint

Lawrence, which eventually led into the Atlantic Ocean. "Music okay?" He glanced at her briefly.

"Uh, sure," she said. Perhaps listening to some quiet music would help relax her. She settled back in her seat and closed her eyes. The strident notes of a fiddle made her start and her eyes flew open. Glancing at Gabe, she saw that he was moving to the lilt and rhythm of the music, and smiling, his fingers tapping with both hands on the wheel. It didn't take her long to recognize the Natalie MacMaster tune. She had seen MacMaster perform "David's Jig" at a concert in Toronto when she had graduated from university. Angel had fallen in love with fiddle music and took every opportunity to go to fairs where fiddlers were featured, especially Cape Breton fiddlers like Natalie and Ashley MacIsaac.

Well, it was not the classical music she had somehow expected Gabe to play, but it was certainly distracting. She found herself tapping her fingers on her thighs, and every once in a while, Gabe would glance her way with a smile, and she would involuntarily smile back. An hour went by surprisingly quickly, and when he turned the music off to inform her that they were approaching Inverness, she felt a twinge in her chest. In another hour they would be arriving at Chéticamp and then crossing to Chéticamp Island. And Gramsy's B&B.

Of course, it was no longer operating as a B&B. Gramsy was the only person who had operated it since her husband died ten years earlier. Her beloved Grampsy, Angel thought, an image of his kind blue eyes, fine white hair and ready smile flashing in her mind.

Gabe turned down the music. "We'll be passing by my restaurant shortly," he said casually. "I studied the culinary arts in Europe and operated my first restaurant in Edinburgh as owner and executive chef. After my parents passed, I returned to Chéticamp Island to take care of the family property. I needed some time away after...their accident."

Yes, Gramsy had tearfully told her all this. "I'm very sorry for your loss." Angel said.

"Thanks," he said huskily. "I ended up staying longer than I first planned, and your grandmother was very supportive." He shot a glance at her. "She helped me a lot in my grief."

Angel bit her lip. *That was Gramsy.* Everybody who knew her always had something to say about her big heart, how she went out of her way to help anyone in need. Gabe had been fortunate to have Gramsy next door to him during such a sad time of loss. Her eyes blurred and she quickly wiped them. Despite her mixed and sometimes resentful feelings toward Gabe these past ten years, she had felt for him and for his parents, who had both been so kind to Angel over the years.

"I'm sorry," Gabe said. "I shouldn't have brought this up."

"No, it's okay," she assured him. "So, you decided to stay?"

"Not right away. I returned to Edinburgh after a month and for the next six months I went back to work." He paused as the rain intensified. When it subsided, he took a deep breath. "Life was very empty without my parents," he said, his voice breaking slightly. "There were too many memories—albeit good ones—but they saddened me. I found myself getting very distracted at the restaurant. Not a good thing for a Michelin chef," he said, shaking his head. "I toyed with the idea of moving to Cape Breton Island, and I finally did. Three years ago. And I opened my second restaurant two years ago. In Inverness." He slowed down as a transport truck zoomed by.

"Yes, Gramsy had mentioned that. And the fact that you've earned a second Michelin star." Angel was surprised that Gabe would open up to her now about such a sensitive time. "Did you sell your restaurant in Scotland?"

"My talented sous-chef is now running it as executive chef while I'm away. I fly out every month or so to check operations."

"What's the name of your restaurant there?"

He met her gaze. "Maeve's." He smiled. "My mother's name."

Angel couldn't help smiling back at his tone of affection. *A loving son.* And he had named his restaurant in Inverness Mara's, after Gramsy. When Gramsy had told her that, and how humbled she felt at having been an inspiration for Gabe over the years, Angel had realized just how much of a connection existed between her and Gabe. Angel had been happy for Gramsy, too, having the support of Gabe, but in all honesty, she had felt a twinge of jealousy at times, knowing that Gabe had the privilege of Gramsy's company and she didn't, teaching full-time, and then too busy with her additional courses to visit Gramsy these past three summers. It made the latent sense of guilt she felt spring up again.

Both Gramsy and Bernadette had shared details of the opening night at Mara's, and how touched Gramsy had been at Gabe's address, thanking her along with his parents for his success as a world-renowned chef.

Gabe stared straight ahead after seeing the sudden look of dismay on Angel's face. Had he said too much? Perhaps he should have been more careful with what he had revealed about himself. There was so much more he wanted and needed to tell Angel, but spilling it in the Range Rover after her tiring flight delay was neither the time nor the place.

Now, they were nearing his restaurant in Inverness, near Cabot Links, one of the world's best golf courses. With the attraction of golf and the scenic ocean views, Mara's had been an instant success when it opened two years ago. "There it is, in the distance." He pointed to a series of rugged cliffs and an architecturally stunning building perched on a flatter stretch of the coastline. "It's hard to see clearly with this rain pelting down, but you can make out the name in lights."

Angel leaned close to the window to try to get a better look. Even when he had redirected the car to continue back on the main road, Angel was still looking out, her arms crossed tightly. And saying nothing.

Seeing Gramsy's name in lights had undoubtedly affected her. It had moved him when he had first seen it. And perhaps she was wondering why Gramsy's business was *his* business. He knew a lot more about Angel than she knew about *him*, simply because he had spent the last three years next door to Gramsy, enjoying many cups of tea and slices of pie or oatcakes with her, and a weekly dinner. From Angel's body language, he sensed he would have to take care in the way he revealed things to her.

"Look, Angel," he said to her back, "there's plenty of time tomorrow and in the week ahead to fill you in about everything. The main thing is that you're here, and shortly we'll be at the B&B." He deliberately avoided saying "we'll be at Gramsy's."

Angel turned away from the window. "I'm tired," she said, in a voice that sounded defeated.

Gabe felt a rush of empathy for her, remembering his feelings after his parents had died. She must be exhausted and overwhelmed. "Don't worry, we're almost there," he said gently, reaching out to tap her arm reassuringly.

She stiffened slightly and he sighed inwardly, turning his gaze back to the road.

As he drove, his thoughts turned back to the grief of his parents' death.

And his broken engagement.

He and Charlotte had dated for four months in what could only be called a "whirlwind" relationship, and were engaged for two months. He had met her at a prestigious charity event she had held at his restaurant, and she had actually been the first one to initiate a second meeting. And then a third. After a few more "meetings," they both agreed that they were officially dating.

She was a high-end real estate agent in Edinburgh, negotiating sales and acquisitions of multimillion condos and the occasional heritage estate. She was impressed with the status of his restaurant and, he discovered later, the economic status of his family. He was initially impressed with her seeming generosity toward charitable causes and, to be honest, with her confidence and beauty. Eyes turned when she walked into a room, drawn to her flaming red hair and glossy red lips. She wore designer clothes, and with her statuesque height enhanced by stiletto heels, people often thought she was a famous model or actress.

Unfortunately, what he believed was genuine about her turned out to be simply a veneer. In the weeks following their official engagement party, an elaborate affair in a Scottish castle, Gabe started to see signs that Charlotte was mostly preoccupied about herself and her needs. A charity event she hosted usually resulted in some benefit for herself, mostly publicity and an increase in clients.

A month into their engagement, Gabe's parents died in a tragic highway accident after their fortieth anniversary cruise, and his life changed instantly. He was overcome with shock, grief and loss, feeling as if he were in a small, rudderless boat in an angry, turbulent ocean. He was overwhelmed with everything he had to do: identify his parents, handle the funeral arrangements and manage his father's business affairs, or designate people who could.

He had no time for flamboyant parties and other social events. In fact, he wanted to hide from the world and try to make sense of what had happened. He ultimately had to take a leave from his restaurant.

Charlotte expressed her sympathies and tried to comfort him, but she couldn't break through the wave of sadness that often submerged him. The outings and trips that she suggested would help him get out of the dark hole of grief, she insisted.

But he wasn't ready. Grief was a process she didn't understand. And it became obvious she wasn't prepared to wait for him to go through the process.

When his doorbell rang one day and he opened it to sign for a package personally addressed to him, he thanked the employee, tipped him and then opened it inside, expecting a sympathy message.

He was right. It was a message from Charlotte, saying she was sorry to have to break their engagement, but she couldn't deal with "the darkness he was stuck in." And she had returned the solitaire in its box.

Gabe realized he was a couple of minutes

away from the B&B. When at last he came down the lane and turned into Gramsy's driveway, Angel straightened, unbuckled her seat belt prematurely and leaned forward to look at the house. Gabe had turned on some indoor lights and the front door lamp lighting up the pathway and steps before he left for the airport. When he came to a stop, Angel burst into tears.

CHAPTER THREE

ANGEL GRATEFULLY TOOK the couple of tissues that Gabe offered her and wiped her face. "Sorry," she murmured.

"You don't need to apologize, Angel. It was only natural that arriving here would trigger your grief."

"Just seeing the lights on and how beautiful the place still is…and knowing Gramsy won't be there to…welcome me…" She felt fresh tears spill onto her cheeks. "It's just too much." She sniffed and wiped her cheeks and nose.

She continued to stare at the house and was glad that Gabe wasn't rushing her out of the car. After a few minutes, she turned to him, "Okay, I'm ready to go in."

He nodded. "I'll get your luggage." He went around to open Angel's door and moments later they were at the front door.

Angel looked past Gabe's shoulder to the bluff and beyond, but it was too dark to see the waters of the Gulf of Saint Lawrence. She could hear the rush of the waves, smell the salt-tinged air and the faint scent of fish emanating from the churned-up waters. The wind had picked up since they had left the diner, and she could hear it rustling the wild grasses bordering the property.

She took a deep breath. She had missed this place, and most of all, Gramsy.

Gabe unlocked the door with a key he said Gramsy had given him, and gave Angel a spare key.

"I'll be okay now," she said, her voice wavering. "Thanks for getting me here."

Gabe nodded, a corner of his mouth lifting. He placed her suitcase inside. "Oh, I almost forgot, I have a bag of homemade muffins I picked up on my way to get you at the airport. I thought you might enjoy them in the morning. I'll go and grab them."

She grudgingly had to admit that Gabe had been very thoughtful, not only with stocking the fridge and turning the house lights on, but also getting her something for breakfast.

"Thanks, I owe you," she said.

Gabe gazed at her for a few seconds. "You don't owe me anything," he said gruffly. "Good night, Angel."

She nodded, afraid that if she replied, she'd burst into tears again, thinking how lonely it would be, the very first night she'd be sleeping in the house without Gramsy.

He left and Angel returned to the kitchen. Feeling somewhat deflated, she plopped down on the cushioned seat of the breakfast nook. She gazed at the familiar decor of the spacious kitchen: the lemon yellow Arborite counters, the deep farmhouse sink with Gramsy's homemade curtains hiding the shelves underneath, the massive oak china cabinet that had belonged to Gramsy's grandmother and in which she proudly displayed plates passed down from their French Acadian ancestors.

There was history here. The history of her ancestors. Her heritage.

A place that soon she'd have to sell. She had no choice. A sob escaped from her lips before she could suppress it.

She suddenly realized that she hadn't heard Gabe starting the car. She hurried to the door window. He was crouched down, inspecting one of the back tires. The only illumination he had was from the porch light. She opened the door, and he looked up.

"Flat," he said. "I'll get it replaced in no time at all and then I'll be out of your hair," he joked.

She shrugged. It was on the tip of her tongue to suggest he walk back to his property and take care of the tire in the morning, but he had already disappeared to get his tools in the trunk. She went back to the kitchen, any previous vestige of fatigue gone. She eyed the kettle. Perhaps a cup of chamomile tea would help relax her and help her sleep tonight...

Angel was startled as an ominous roll of thunder reverberated around her, followed moments later by large raindrops that slammed the large picture window like projectiles. Her thoughts turned immediately to Gabe. He'd be getting drenched.

She rushed to the front door as a series of lightning flashes illuminated the sky and the rain soaking Gabe. Opening the door quickly, she called out, "Gabe! Come inside!"

Gramsy would surely have extended the hand of friendship and invited Gabe or anyone else in, out of the rain. How could she expect him to walk back to his place in this kind of weather? It wasn't as if their homes were the traditional distance apart, like city homes. Each of their properties was a couple of acres, and walking from the B&B to Gabe's estate was downright dangerous under these conditions.

He sprinted over and closed the door behind him. "Good timing," he said wryly. "If the weather forecast is correct, things are going to get even nastier in the next few hours." As if on cue, the wind shrieked through a partially opened window in the kitchen and Angel ran to close it. She grabbed a roll of paper towels and mopped up the water on the sill and floor.

She quickly returned to the foyer, then glanced at Gabe, standing in the foyer, his hair and shoulders dripping. The paper towel roll in her hand wouldn't do.

"Um, why don't you hang up your jacket here in the foyer, and then grab a towel or two in the washroom and dry your curly locks. I'll put on some tea."

Did she just say "curly locks"? Good lord.

His eyebrows lifted and his mouth curled in amusement. "I thought you'd never ask," he quipped, removing his shoes.

When he returned, the kettle was whistling, and she had the mugs and muffins out on the breakfast nook by the picture window overlooking the gulf. The only view they had, though, was of the rain still battering the windowpanes.

He sifted through the boxes of tea Angel had set out, his blue-green eyes narrowing as he contemplated his choices. Angel's heart did a flip, his damp hair and T-shirt evoking memories of swimming together and then returning to this very nook for a snack and a cool drink.

With Gabe sitting across from her, as he had done countless times before, Angel felt surprisingly at ease. And relieved, to be honest, not to be alone in Gramsy's house. Not because she was afraid; it was just that being there by herself would somehow make the emptiness of the place more palpable.

Things would be different in the light of day. Not that her feelings of sadness and emptiness would magically disappear, but at least the light might mitigate her sense of loneliness and grief.

"Hmm, I'll have the wild blueberry tea," Gabe said with a smile across from her. He surveyed the muffins. "Lemon cranberry, blueberry, carrot and oatmeal raisin. After you, miss."

"Easy choice. Lemon cranberry. And you?"

"Carrot. I can't resist the cream cheese icing. It tastes like the cake Gramsy..." He paused, and Angel could see from his furrowed brows that he wasn't sure if he should bring up memories about Gramsy, in case it incited more tears.

"Used to make," Angel said lightly. "I had forgotten about that." She peeled off the paper and bit into her muffin. "Very good. Thanks."

Gabe nodded. "Well, they *were* supposed to be for breakfast. By the way, I picked up some bread, eggs and milk for you earlier. All in the fridge."

"Thanks, and for the apples and bananas on the counter, too. That was nice of you."

"I'm generally a nice guy," he said with a

crooked smile. He ran one hand through his hair. "My curly locks are pretty dry now," he said wryly. He plopped the last bite of his muffin in his mouth and stood up. "Thank you for the tea." He glanced at his watch. "I'd better get going."

Angel's gaze flew to the round clock on the wall and she did a double take. It was almost midnight. "But it's still raining."

"It's a warm rain. I'll be fine."

She put her hands on her hips. "I'll not be responsible for you getting struck by lightning, Gabriel McKellar."

His brows arched at her use of his full name. "I jog every day," he said, unable to stop himself from grinning. "I'll just jog faster. Besides, it looks like the thunder and lightning have stopped." He put on his jacket and reached into his pocket. Handing her his business card, he said, "Call me if you need anything, Angel. Anytime.

"I hope you get some rest," he said, his tone now serious. "I'll be in touch." Gabe opened the door and a violent swirl of wind and rain hurled the door back along with a deafening roll of thunder. Letting out a cry, Angel grabbed Gabe's arm as he grabbed the handle and shut the door quickly.

The wind had whipped his hood back and her gaze went from the hair she had caressed more than once ages ago to the teal eyes that could sometimes be as enigmatic as the dark gulf waters. She realized her hand was still clasping his arm and she started to pull it away, but he stopped her, taking her hand in his.

Her heart stood still as he searched her face, and then started drumming when their gazes locked.

"Okay, that settles that, then." He inhaled and exhaled deeply. "I'm afraid I'm going to have to ask you if there's room at the inn for me tonight," he said gruffly, his Scottish brogue sending a flutter through her.

Gabe watched Angel processing his words: her eyebrows lifting, her mouth dropping open and then closing, her intense brown eyes and the touch of her hand in his sending shock waves through him. "Let me rephrase that. If you insist on barring me from leaving, I can just camp out on the living room couch, if that's okay."

Angel shook her head as if coming out of a trance. She forced herself to pull her hand away from his. "No. I mean yes, of course it's okay. And no, not on the couch, for goodness' sakes. Gramsy would not approve. You can take either one of the guest rooms with an en suite upstairs." Her gaze flew to the puddle at his feet. "Stay right there. I'll grab some towels."

He watched her disappear into the bathroom past the foyer and reemerge with two large towels. He removed his jacket and shoes and used one towel for the floor and one for his face and hair.

She reached over to lock the door and then turned on the light of the stairway leading to the bedrooms. "I'm sure there's everything you need up there." Her brows furrowed. "Gramsy provided guest robes in the B&B rooms. You can—um—change into one of them and use the upstairs laundry room if you need to."

"Thanks. I really appreciate it." He smiled. "I'll thank you properly with a meal at my restaurant. Whenever you're up for it."

Angel held up a hand. "No worries. You don't have to." She turned slightly. "I'll just check out a few things down here and then… I'll be calling it a night." She gestured toward the stairway. "The guest rooms are the first ones on the right at the top of the stairs. Good night."

"Good night, Angel." He watched her return to the kitchen.

Upstairs, he found the luxurious robe, hanging ready for the next guest. He put it on, reminded of how efficient and thoughtful Gramsy had been as a B&B hostess. There was no need that her guests might have had that *she* hadn't thought about first. And generously provided, as promised on her website. Not just the usual items that might have been forgotten, like toothbrushes and toothpaste, but other things that provided a special touch: a welcome basket with snacks and drinks, a plush towel that they could leave with, that she had embroidered with their initials, discount coupons for attractions and restaurants, including his, and a souvenir book about the special attractions of Chéticamp and Cape Breton Island. It was no wonder that many of her guests returned. Or spread the word. The guest rooms were very rarely unoccupied.

His hair dry and his jeans hanging over the towel rack in the washroom—he didn't want to start the dryer at this late hour—Gabe walked to the large window of the bedroom and gazed out toward the gulf. The boughs of the apple trees on the property were swaying wildly. Intermittent flashes of lightning revealed the undulating wild grasses and the churning waters, with whitecaps forming and collapsing. Such weather wasn't uncommon at this time of year, a result of the seasonal storms south of the border and swirling off the coast of Florida. Unfortunately, it was a rough start to Angel's return to Chéticamp.

Yawning, he sauntered away from the window, removed his robe and settled comfortably under the covers of the king-size bed. He turned off the lamp on the night table and stared up at the ceiling. It had been a full day for him, not just because of the long drive to the airport and then back, but also because of the anticipation of meeting Angel again. He had not seen her in person in ten years, but he still recalled times spent with her and her friend Bernadette. Gramsy had mentioned her countless times since he'd moved back to the island.

He knew that Evangeline was the name she was given at birth, but her parents tended to shorten it to Angel most times. *Unless they were being serious with her,* Gramsy laughed, *and giving her time out.*

While enjoying a cup of tea with Gramsy, she always seemed to find a way of bringing up Angel and would proudly show him photos of her, past and present. He learned about her graduation from teachers college, her new apartment and the additional courses she was taking these past three years. So, he knew exactly what she looked like since he had last seen her ten years ago. She was beautiful. Beautiful with sad brown eyes that reminded him of the innocent gaze of a fawn. They were eyes that reflected her grief for her beloved grandmother. And there was something more that he had glimpsed in their depths. Regret, and possibly guilt.

Gramsy had told him that Angel felt bad about

staying away for the past three summers. "I miss my darling girl," she told Gabe, "but I understand, and I told her that."

Gabe could understand Angel's feeling remorseful for not being around in the last years of Gramsy's life. He had felt similar regrets when his parents had passed, wishing he had spent more time with them instead of being so wrapped up in his restaurant. The sad thing for Angel was that she had finally booked her flight and visit to Chéticamp Island after finishing her extra courses, but Gramsy's heart had given out a couple of weeks before Angel's arrival.

A series of squeaks in the oak floor alerted Gabe to Angel's presence in the hall outside his room. And then a door opening and closing. The last thing she'd probably expected was to have her childhood playmate and first boyfriend sleeping under the same roof on her first night back.

He closed his eyes. He was kind of glad it had turned out that way. Perhaps his presence made Angel's first night at Gramsy's a little bit easier for her.

Gabe turned to one side and flipped over his pillow. Ordinarily, he didn't have a problem getting to sleep right away once his head hit the pillow. He just hoped Angel would be able to sleep well in the few hours left before sunrise.

CHAPTER FOUR

ANGEL TURNED ON the light switch of her bedroom and set down her suitcase. She slowly scanned the room that Gramsy had always reserved for her: The wallpaper with its delicate design of roses against a soft leaf green background; the cushioned window seat from where she could reach out and grab a Granny Smith apple from the edge of one of the massive trees that had been planted decades earlier by her grandparents; the antique white four-poster bed with its light pink bedspread and a folded quilt over the footboard that Gramsy had recently finished, each square consisting of a piece of Angel's clothes from summer visits over the years. In one of their last chats before Angel went on her cruise, Gramsy had proudly shown her the quilt and Angie had been moved to tears.

And now her eyes blurred again. She wiped them with a corner of her shirtsleeve. "Oh, Gramsy," she murmured, "I wish you were still here. I'm going to miss you so much." She walked over and sat on the edge of the bed, pressing the quilt against her cheek. She sniffled as her gaze fell on the plush toy lying next to the pillow sham. Her white, well-loved unicorn, with its shiny horn and rainbow-colored mane and tail. Angel couldn't help laughing. She had called it "Magic" and she had slept with it often as a child, after Gramsy had read her a bedtime story, and even later, when she was reading fairy tales by herself after Gramsy had kissed her good-night and gone to bed.

Angel sighed. The flight delay, meeting Gabe, the drive and all her thoughts and emotions throughout the day and night had left her exhausted. She had to try to get some sleep, strange though it might feel with Gabe in the room across the hall.

She fished out her nightgown from her suitcase, and after changing she flicked off the light and slipped under the covers. Sleep eluded her but she kept her eyes closed and tried to focus on listening to the rain and wind thrumming against her windows. Images of Gabe flashed in her mind despite her best intentions: The height of him as she craned her neck to meet his gaze at the car rental office; his teal-green eyes softening when he mentioned Gramsy's carrot cake; his upper body swaying to the fiddle music while driving; his damp hair with its curling ends; and those enigmatic ocean eyes as he asked if there was room for him at the inn.

And then imagining him in a guest robe...

The sunlight flooding her room woke Angel up. She squinted and waited until her eyes had adjusted somewhat and then opened them fully. Her gaze flew to the window. Droplets of rain dotted the panes, but there was no active rain that she could see.

Angel checked the time on her phone. *What? How could it be 9:10?* She scrambled out of bed. Was Gabe still here? She caught sight of herself in the dresser mirror. If he was, she could *not* go downstairs until she showered and felt more human. She grabbed the robe hanging on the back of her door. It brought a lump to her throat, knowing Gramsy had put it there in anticipation of her arrival, along with the fresh towels on the long, cushioned bench at the foot of her bed.

She opened her door slightly. Gabe's door was half open. Had he left? Debating whether she should make a dash to the bathroom, the sound of clinking dishes and cutlery downstairs answered her question. She stepped into the bathroom separating her room from Gramsy's and rushed through her shower. After briskly towel-drying her hair, she tied the bathrobe tightly around her waist and opened the door. Startled at the sight of Gabe coming up the stairs, she froze, self-conscious about her disheveled hair and robe.

"Good morning, Angel," he said pleasantly, as if it were perfectly natural to be meeting her coming out of the shower. He paused on the second last step. "I hope you slept well."

"I did, thanks," she said. "Longer than I thought I would. Um… I'll be down shortly."

He nodded. "I hope you don't mind? I took the liberty of getting a few things together for breakfast. I was just coming up to see if you… if everything was okay."

Angel wasn't sure how she should respond. Gabe was obviously quite comfortable in Gramsy's house. She wasn't sure *she* was as comfortable with having him linger in the spaces she thought she would be lingering through alone, going from room to room and coming to terms with Gramsy's absence. But she had no intention of being rude and asking him to leave, given his generosity in taking the time to drive all the way to the airport to pick her up and bring her here. Besides, he would probably leave right after breakfast to deal with his flat tire. "I'm fine." *For the moment.* "I'll be down in a couple of minutes."

She walked into her room without waiting to hear him reply and closed the door firmly. Her heart was thudding. During the time that Gabe had stood there with his muscled arms crossed, his hair damp too, his T-shirt and jeans fitting him perfectly, she actually felt that he belonged there even more than she did. A strange feeling, and a perplexing one.

There were a lot of questions she wanted—*needed*—to ask him, but she would have to find the right time to do so. *Not today.* Today she just wanted to be alone in the house with her feelings and memories of Gramsy.

Angel opened her suitcase and sifted through the few clothes she had decided to bring: some casual, and a couple of more formal items for the reception that would be happening in two weeks' time in memory of Gramsy. It was her friend Bernadette who had called with the devastating news of Gramsy's passing. They had talked and cried over shared memories for at least an hour, and Bernadette had told her that she would drop in the day after Angel arrived in Chéticamp.

She would call Bernadette later, she decided, as she fished out a pair of fuchsia Capris and a pale yellow eyelet blouse and quickly changed. She brushed her hair back in a ponytail and added a bit of blush to her pale cheeks.

The welcome aroma of coffee greeted her as she walked downstairs. She noticed Gabe's gaze sweeping over her as she entered the kitchen and, feeling her cheeks ignite, she wished she hadn't even bothered to use blush.

Gabe had the breakfast nook set up with breakfast dishes, juice glasses, milk jug and mugs. He filled a mug and handed it to her.

"Thanks," she said. "I can't start my day without coffee."

"Enjoy." He smiled. "And shortly, breakfast will be served." He gestured toward a pan on the stove and a bowl beside it.

Angel watched him as he proceeded to make scrambled eggs, bacon and toast. Her mouth started to water as the aroma of bacon pervaded the kitchen.

"Is there anything more tantalizing than the smell and sound of sizzling bacon?" He grinned, and a few minutes later handed Angel a plate with a generous portion of both eggs and bacon, a couple of tomato slices and two slices of toasted and buttered sourdough bread. "Enjoy. I'll make mine and join you in a minute." He took a drink of his coffee and turned again to the stove.

"Thanks, I will," she said, and after her first few bites, "Why does food always taste better when someone else makes it?"

Gabe chuckled. "I don't know. Especially since I'm usually the one making the food."

It was obvious that Gabe was very much at

home in Gramsy's kitchen. Gramsy had mentioned his treating her with one of his signature dishes every so often. Angel couldn't help wondering if Gabe currently had a girlfriend that he enjoyed cooking for. He must be attached; she couldn't imagine that someone with his striking good looks and culinary expertise could be single.

A couple of minutes later, he was eating across from her. She gazed at his left hand. *No ring.* But that didn't necessarily mean anything. And not that it was any of her business.

"Is something wrong?"

Angel realized that she had stopped eating and Gabe had caught her staring at his hand. "Um, no, I was just thinking…" she murmured and promptly turned her attention back to the remaining food on her plate.

"About what?" Gabe persisted.

"Um…" What could she say? That she was wondering if he was married or with someone? "I was thinking about calling Bernadette," she said quickly. It was true, after all. "She said she would come by later."

"Ah, my sister from another mother," he said jokingly. "She keeps me in line, that one."

"As someone should," she blurted.

Gabe laughed. "Now you sound like her. That's a compliment," he added quickly with a wink. "Bernie's a true Cape Bretoner, speaking her mind. And often."

He rose. "Well, I should be going before my mouth gets me in more trouble," he said. "I need to look after that tire. But first, I want to thank you, Angel," he said. "For allowing me to stay at the inn.'"

Angel set down her fork. "It wouldn't have been very nice of me to have you walk—or jog—to your place in such bad weather. Gramsy wouldn't have approved. Anyway, thank *you* for making breakfast," she said. "I should have set my alarm."

"No worries, Angel. I always enjoy cooking." He started to walk away and then stopped to gaze back at her. "I imagine you want to stay put and settle in today. When you're ready to go over a few matters Gramsy wanted me to discuss with you, just call me or text." He gestured toward the counter where she had left his card. "What about the lawyer?" She felt herself tensing.

"We'll tackle things with him later. It doesn't have to be today. Or tomorrow. It's important that I talk to you first."

He was being enigmatic and Angel wasn't motivated to pry for more details. Not now. Maybe not even later today. She would see how she felt after reconnecting with Gramsy's house on her own.

"Good luck with your car," she said casually. "I'll let you know."

Gabe nodded. "If you're up for a good walk, you're also welcome to meet me at my place. When you're ready." Without waiting for her to answer, he strode across the kitchen to the foyer. Moments later, he was gone.

After replacing his tire with the "donut" in the trunk, Gabe drove straight to the auto repair shop to have the tire replaced with a new one. On the drive home, he reflected on the feelings Angel must be experiencing. He understood perfectly that she needed time to process being back in Gramsy's home. With Gramsy gone, it was no longer operating as a B&B, as the only staff had been Gramsy as owner, manager and cook; a younger woman whom Gramsy had hired after Angel's grandfather died to do the cleaning and housework relating to the B&B; and a gardener to maintain the property. Everything else, Gramsy had managed on her own.

So, Angel didn't have to worry about having to deal with guests. The "Gramsy's B&B" sign was still up, but word of Gramsy's passing and the closing of the place had circulated in and around the community.

What Angel didn't know—yet—was that Gramsy, discovering that she had some health concerns a year ago, had been astute and forward-thinking, making plans and updating her will. She had decided not to let Angel know about her irregular heartbeat and subsequent tests, angiogram and, ultimately, three stents until Angel arrived at the beginning of August, when her last course was done. Sadly, her heart hadn't lasted that long.

He would have to explain all this to Angel, and why Gramsy had confided in *him* instead of her.

There was a lot that Angel didn't know about him.

Their lives had intersected many times over the years when Angel returned to the island in the summer. His summer visits were often spent bicycling over to Gramsy's. She was an awesome neighbor and had invited him and his parents for dinner quite regularly, and they had done the same. On one occasion, his parents couldn't make it but sent him, and Gramsy had handed him an apron and encouraged him to help make the meal.

He smiled at the memory of sautéing Digby scallops and adding chopped parsley and lemon zest, and drizzling them with some of the lemon juice, and a shot of white wine or chicken broth. The next time, she had him help her with all the steps of making rappie pie, which she told him was the national dish of Nova Scotia and Prince Edward Island Acadians.

Gramsy enjoyed his company and encouraged his culinary curiosity and appreciation for island traditions. And because she hadn't been blessed with a grandson, she mentioned with a twinkle in her eye, she was happy to symbolically adopt him as her grandson. *So now I have two grandkids,* she chuckled. *And you can call me Gramsy, too.*

Gabe didn't really know how much Gramsy had told Angel over the years about him. He imagined he'd soon find out.

He stepped out of the Range Rover and once inside his house, he strode to the floor-to-ceiling living room window, where he could gaze out at the stretch of beach and Gramsy's adjoining property. The sky was a palette of blues and grays, with a smattering of small white clouds. The gulf waters reflected the same hues, and although the wind had calmed from the evening before, it was still ruffling the waters enough to produce whitecaps.

Turning away from the window, his gaze fell on a framed photo of his parents on the coffee table. It had been taken at their thirtieth-anniversary dinner. Gabe sank back on the dark brown leather sectional and felt a lump begin to form in his throat. He felt their loss acutely, and when he'd returned to Chéticamp Island, Gramsy was there for him, enveloping him with all the love and support that he needed in his time of grief and mourning.

And now she was gone, too.

He understood how vulnerable and lost Angel must feel now. Gramsy had told him that Angel had lost her father from a stroke when she was twenty-one, and her mother had passed from cancer five years ago. Gramsy was her last living relative, and they had been very close. And Angel, like him, had no siblings she could turn to for support.

He hoped that she would continue to accept the support he was ready to give her.

CHAPTER FIVE

ANGEL DID THE few breakfast dishes by hand. As she watched the soapy water swirl down the drain, she felt the absence of Gabe disquieting. Which was strange, given that she had initially wanted to be alone in Gramsy's home. Drying her hands, she sighed and glanced around. It was going to be hard, going from room to room, reminiscing about times spent here. But it was something she had to do. *Wanted* to do. She wanted to cling to every memory, lock it securely in her heart and mind. In fact, she planned to take a photo of each room, to remember how it was when Gramsy was alive, since she would have to ultimately sell the place.

That would be a sad ending to Gramsy's B&B, a fixture in the community for decades. Angel hoped that maybe there would be someone local who might be interested in purchasing it and continuing to operate it as a B&B.

Selling it would break her heart, but she had no other option. She couldn't see herself packing up and moving from her Toronto neighborhood to relocate to Cape Breton Island and take over the B&B. Much as the place held treasured memories since her childhood, there was no way she could just give up her teaching job and start a new life on the East Coast. *Year-round.*

Sighing again, Angel scanned the kitchen, probably her favorite room in the house. The room that diffused Gramsy's mouthwatering breakfast scents up to her bedroom and lured her downstairs. The kitchen island where Gramsy let her help with making her many varieties of cookies and fudge, not to mention her oatcakes, pies and puddings.

This triggered a particular memory: racing around the apple trees on the property with a visiting neighbor—*Gabe*—and then the two of them using a broom to knock down some of the ripe apples. After filling the sturdy wicker baskets Gramsy had supplied them with, they raced back to her kitchen, and later that evening, they enjoyed a slice of pie fresh out of the oven, with a scoop of vanilla ice cream on top.

And then, while Gramsy relaxed in her favorite recliner, she and Gabe would pretend to own the B&B and cook for the guests. Angel blinked. When was the last time she had even conjured up *that* memory? Well, part of it had come true, with Gabe becoming a renowned chef and cooking not only at his restaurants, but for her in this very kitchen. As for her owning the B&B, she couldn't see that happening.

Angel sauntered into the living room, eyeing the soft, sage green couch where she had loved to curl up on with a book. It looked out onto the gulf and was the perfect spot to feel cozy in during a summer storm. She gazed at the corner bookshelf that still held all of Gramsy's books and some of her own. *Classic Fairy Tales. Anne of Green Gables. Heidi. The Secret Garden.* And later additions: *Little Women* and a number of Agatha Christie and Jane Austen novels. Gramsy never booked guests during Angel's stays, but any other time, they were welcome to read any of the books in this common room.

Her gaze fell on the spine of a book gifted to her on her sixteenth birthday: *Evangeline*, Henry Wadsworth Longfellow's epic poem published in 1847, chronicling the expulsion of the Acadians in Nova Scotia by the British and New England authorities from 1755 to 1764. She had been moved by the story of the French farmers and fishermen of the area being deported from Acadie, and in particular, the heartbreaking separation of an Acadian girl, Evangeline, from her beloved fiancé, Gabriel, and her search for him for years before reuniting with him on his deathbed.

Angel had wept over their sad destiny, and she wondered at a love so strong that would compel a woman to spend years searching to find her lover. She was captivated by the 1920 bronze sculpture of Evangeline in the Grand-Pré National Historic Site in central Nova Scotia on one of her subsequent summer visits, and had reread the poem so many times that certain passages remained in her memory. She had also driven along the scenic Evangeline Trail, the historic route through the Annapolis Valley, where the French first settled in North America, and ending in Yarmouth on the southwest coast of Nova Scotia.

Angel felt goose bumps on her arms now at her recollection of the first lines of the poem: *This is the forest primeval. The murmuring pines and the hemlocks, Bearded with moss, and in garments green, indistinct in the twilight, Stand like Druids of eld, with voices sad and prophetic... Loud from its rocky caverns, the deep-voiced neighboring ocean Speaks...*

Angel sighed and sank into one corner of the couch. When she was younger, her parents had told her that they had named *her* Evangeline, moved by the spirit of the fictional character who symbolized the deportation and the fortitude and persistence of the Acadians. Since her mom and dad always considered her their "little angel," the name stuck early on, and Angel only heard her parents call her Evangeline when they were being firm with her about something.

We have our own Evangeline and Gabriel, she'd overheard her mom say to Gabe's mother over tea at Angel's birthday when Maeve had spotted the book in the living room. She and Gabe had just finished having cake and were heading out for a stroll on the beach.

What was that all about? Gabe had asked her when they had reached the beach.

Angel told him about the Acadian lovers and their destiny as they walked, and for a few moments he was silent. When he stopped suddenly, she gazed up at him and the look in his eyes made her heart begin to hammer softly. He had never looked at her that way before. And then he had fished a box out of the back pocket of his jeans and handed it to her.

"Happy birthday, Angel."

She opened it wordlessly and lifted out a heart-shaped pink shell with a tiny hole in it. She turned it over and saw his initial, as he marked other shells he had given her. But next to this initial, he had inscribed an *x* and an *o*. Underneath the shell was a delicate gold chain. He attached the shell to it, and she let him place it around her neck. Her heart was racing now, and as he turned her gently around and leaned forward, she found herself looking up to meet his kiss. A sweet kiss that took her breath away. And then another, and another.

Angel stood up abruptly, berating herself silently for resurrecting memories that ultimately generated feelings of sadness and loss. She proceeded to walk through every room on the main floor, recalling instead a special memory that involved Gramsy. Sometimes she laughed out loud, and sometimes a few tears slipped out. She continued her tour on the second floor, through the guest rooms and, finally, to Gramsy's room.

Angel sat on the corner of Gramsy's bed. And was flooded. Memories of running into the room in the morning and jumping into bed with Gramsy. Tickling her when Gramsy pretended to be sleeping still. She placed her palms on the quilt Gramsy had made and looked around at all the familiar things that made this room so special: the antique dressing table with the round mirror where Angel had sat while Gramsy brushed Angel's long hair with a silver brush; the huge wardrobe that reminded Angel of the one in *The Lion, the Witch and the Wardrobe*; and her bookshelf with all sorts of intriguing titles.

What was going to happen to all these treasured belongings of Gramsy? And the B&B?

Angel felt a surge of anxiety. She put a hand up to her heart, which had started to race. Lying back on the bed and closing her eyes, she focused on doing her deep-breathing exercises to help her relax. When her anxiety had diminished, Angel turned on one side and hugged Gramsy's pillow.

"I love you, Gramsy," she murmured, her heart heavy. "I'm going to miss you."

The sharp ring of the doorbell startled her, and she jumped up, momentarily disoriented. She glanced at her watch and realized she had drifted off. She rushed downstairs.

Had Gabe forgotten something? Her heart thumped at the thought of seeing him again. When she reached the foyer and peered through the side window, the sight of the figure standing at the doorstep made her eyes prickle. She flung open the door and fell into the embrace of her longtime friend Bernadette, whom she hadn't expected until later.

"Oh, Angel, I'm so sorry about Gramsy," Bernadette said, her voice catching in a sob.

Angel nodded and let her own tears flow for a few moments. "I know," she sniffed. "I feel so bad I didn't get back in time—"

"Angel, Gramsy wouldn't want you to feel bad," Bernadette said, squeezing Angel's shoulders. "She understood why you were away. And she was so looking forward to your visit this summer." She gave Angel another hug. "Who was to know that her beautiful heart would give out?" She shook her head sympathetically. "These things are out of everyone's control…"

"I know," Angel said, wiping her eyes. "Come on, let's go in."

She made tea while Bernadette sat at the island and caught her up with news of her family and work. She was head waitress at Making Waves, a popular seafood restaurant on the northwest coast of Cape Breton Island. She had moved to Halifax for a few years, working for her certification in the restaurant and hospitality industry, and had recently moved back to Chéticamp.

From the first time they had met as children, Angel and Bernadette had become fast friends, and when Angel was back home, they became pen pals and looked forward to reuniting for a few weeks every summer. "Mmm, peach," Bernadette said, and smiled. "You remembered."

Angel nodded and sat across from her. "Of course. How could I forget anything about my peachy friend?" They both laughed and Angel was glad for these moments of levity, and grateful that she would have Bernadette close by this week.

"Okay, now tell me more about your *friend*," Angel said. Bernadette had been dating a real estate agent for the last three months. Ross Grant was an islander and very successful at his job. Bernadette had shared that he was a widower with no kids. Sadly, his wife had passed suddenly from a rare heart condition five years earlier.

Her eyes widened at Bernadette's grin. "Wait, what? Are you two serious?"

Bernadette's eyes seemed to sparkle. "I... *Yes!* He's not like any of the guys I dated in the past. He's thoughtful, smart, funny and—" she winked "—as cute as hell."

"I'm so happy for you, Bernie," Angel cried, rushing over to give Bernadette a tight hug. "I can't wait to meet him."

Bernadette nodded. "You will tonight. He and I are taking you out for dinner."

Angel's smile faded. "I...um... That's very kind, but I don't think I'm up to going out in public. Sorry."

Bernadette reached out and clasped Angel's hand. "Don't apologize. I understand. Okay, how about I order and have it delivered here?"

Angel couldn't help but concede at Bernadette's hopeful expression. "Sure, I can handle that." She narrowed her eyes deliberately. "Besides, I have to meet this man of yours and make sure he's worthy of my bestie."

Bernadette laughed. "By the way, Angel,

how did everything go with Gabe yesterday? He stopped by the restaurant a couple of nights ago and told me he would be picking you up."

Angel shrugged nonchalantly. "Yeah, he took it upon himself to cancel my car rental and meet me himself," she said. "He said he was following Gramsy's wishes."

Bernadette nodded. "I'm not surprised. Gabe and Gramsy have gotten pretty close over the years, especially after his parents died."

Angel frowned. She remembered feeling sad when Gramsy had shared the news of the terrible accident that had claimed the lives of Gabe's parents. They had always been very kind to her. "I'm sure that Gramsy would have been a great support for him," Angel murmured. "She was always like a mother hen to anyone in the community who was grieving, making meals and comforting them in any way she could."

"Yup," Bernadette nodded. "And Gabe never forgot it." Her phone trilled and she read the text. She quickly replied and then put the phone down. "It was Ross—" she smiled "—asking about you. He said he'd order and meet me here. You and I don't have to do a thing."

"That's very kind. Thanks. He scores a point in my books," she teased.

"What about Gabe?" Bernadette countered.

Angel threw her a puzzled look. "What do you mean?"

"Did he make any sort of impression?" Bernadette said casually. "I mean, you haven't seen him for ten years."

"What kind of impression was he supposed to make? I mean, I did notice he was impossibly tall…"

"And?"

Angel put a finger to her temple and tapped it, as if trying to remember. "Oh yes. He had two eyes and ears, a nose and a mouth." She stared pointedly at Bernadette. "What's your point, Bernie?"

Bernadette shrugged innocently. "I just wondered if you had noticed how good-looking he is."

Angel's lips twitched. "No," she replied emphatically.

"Liar," Bernadette shot back with a grin.

Gabe decided to go for a jog after ending a long business call to his restaurant manager and acting executive chef in Edinburgh. He changed into a long-sleeved hoodie and sweatpants, and moments later he was breathing the fresh ocean air and enjoying the brisk wind that was prevalent at this time of year. It wasn't the aggressive wind of the night before, and if the week's weather forecast was to be believed, the wind would again rise up and show its less pleasant side, influenced by the yearly hurricane activity swirling off the Florida coast.

For now, it was perfect jogging weather. He usually went for at least five miles every morning, depending on how busy his day was. His restaurant opened for lunch, but his shift started at 5:00 p.m., so he usually arrived at three to prep for the evening with his sous-chef and staff.

As he passed his property and continued along the coast in the direction opposite Gramsy's land, he wondered how Angel was doing. He knew from his chat with Bernadette a couple of days ago that she would be dropping by to be with Angel today. He had also told her that he would be picking up Angel at the airport. Bernadette's eyebrows had shot up and he explained that when Gramsy learned the details of Angel's flight schedule a month ago, she told him that she didn't want Angel driving for hours after her flight.

My poor girl will be exhausted enough after finishing her course. Gramsy had advised him to cancel Angel's car rental—she had the confirmation number that Angel had given her, along with her flight schedule—and to just show up. And then she texted him a recent photo of Angel.

Gabe had looked at the photo often in the

weeks preceding the day of Angel's flight. It hadn't been the first photo Gramsy had shared with him, proclaiming her pride for her only granddaughter. He had seen photos of Angel over the years: wearing braces in her teen years; beaming in her sea-green prom gown, her hair done up, with tendrils on either side of her cheeks, standing next to her smug-looking date; graduating from university and teachers college; and countless birthdays.

During his teatime visits with Gramsy, their conversation would inevitably veer to Angel's accomplishments with her students, and other events in her life.

Like her dates.

Angel would probably be embarrassed, to say the least, that Gramsy would have shared any details about her dates to him or anyone else. Not that any of those meager details had been worthy of embarrassment.

Gramsy had simply dismissed the guys based on what Angel had told her. Which wasn't much, she complained to Gabe with a laugh. *He was too arrogant. He ate like a slob. His gaze wandered to other women.* In their last teatime together, Gramsy had expressed her hope that now that Angel had finished her special courses, she would hopefully go out more and find a special guy.

The recent photo was the only one Gramsy

had texted to him, and he couldn't help scrolling to view it every day. The sun was shining on Angel's dark auburn hair, and she was laughing, her bright red lipstick matching her top above rolled-up jeans and bare feet. It was taken at a beach northwest of Toronto, Gramsy told him.

Angel's dark brown eyes looked almost teasing, and Gabe wondered if the person taking the photo was someone special that maybe Angel hadn't told Gramsy about.

An inner voice warned Gabe to put a halt to those thoughts. This was a sad and sensitive time for Angel. Gramsy wanted him to be there for Angel and to help her with the decisions that had to be made around the B&B. Angel was vulnerable and Gramsy trusted *him* to see that her affairs were carried out the way she intended.

Gabe checked his watch and saw that it was time to turn back. The wind was starting to pick up and the sky was changing from hues of blue to gray. He took a drink from his water bottle and then headed back. When he was about a quarter of a mile from his place, he caught sight of someone walking along the beach, just past his property. A few minutes later, he realized it was Angel. He slowed down and stopped a few yards away. He had worked up a sweat and took a moment to grab a small towel in his hoodie pocket to wipe his brow. He breathed in and out deeply, hoping to slow his pulse, which he knew wasn't just the result of his jog.

"Hi, Angel."

"Hello."

Gabe nodded. Up to now, she had never called him by name. An image flashed in his mind of the photo of Angel that Gramsy had texted to him. Her eyes weren't sparkling now and she wasn't laughing, but he still found her beautiful. She was wearing fuchsia Capris and a yellow blouse, and her hair was up in a casual ponytail. A natural beauty.

"Are you starting or ending your walk?"

"Ending. Bernadette came by for a bit and then kindly offered to get some groceries for me."

He nodded. "Nice of her. Can I offer you tea or a refreshing drink at my place, since we're practically on my doorstep?"

CHAPTER SIX

GABE'S TEAL-GREEN eyes were mesmerizing. His hair was windswept and damp, and yes, even in his hoodie and sweatpants, Angel couldn't deny that he was good-looking. *Damned* good-looking.

But she had no intention of letting him know that she thought that about him. And she really shouldn't take him up on his offer. She still felt vulnerable and wasn't ready to show her feelings again to Gabe. Bursting into tears when they arrived at the B&B had been regrettable, and she couldn't be sure that any mention of Gramsy while they were having tea wouldn't incite the same response.

She had to try to curb her emotions, at least when she was with Gabe or the lawyer. How could she make rational decisions about Gramsy's affairs if she allowed herself to be openly overwhelmed with grief? The meeting with the three of them was scheduled for the day after tomorrow, and Angel meant to present a staunch demeanor. She had to be strong. She needed some time before then to condition herself for the meeting. If she had to cry and break down, she would do it in the privacy of Gramsy's house. And with Bernadette, with whom she had had a connection for years.

"Angel?"

Startling, she realized that she had been staring beyond Gabe at the undulating waters of the gulf. She shifted her gaze back to him. "Um, thanks, but I'll have to pass. I need to—"

"You don't need to explain, Angel." He scanned the sky. "From the look of those clouds and whitecaps, I think we may be in for another blast of bad weather." He started to turn away. "Take care."

She nodded and kept walking. A sudden gust of wind sent up a spray of sand. She shielded her face as she headed for the path to Gramsy's. The first onslaught of rain followed moments later and at the rumbling of thunder, she started to run. Her foot made contact with something protruding in the sand. She catapulted forward and cried out as she felt a sharp item puncturing her lower leg as she landed unceremoniously on the beach, her face grazing the sand.

She winced as she shifted her position and managed to sit up.

"Don't move, Angel," Gabe said, reaching her. "Did you hit your head?"

"I—I don't think so. It happened so fast." She brushed the sand from her face. "My leg—" She gasped at the gash on her blood-splattered limb.

Gabe frowned. "Here, let me wrap that up for now." He pulled a small towel out of his hoodie pocket and tied it around the wound and her calf. "I'll clean it up at the house. Sit tight for a minute." He scanned the beach sand around her and extracted a piece of driftwood with a nail sticking out of it and a tattered piece of cloth attached to the head of the nail. "A kid's sailboat," he said, shaking his head.

"I think I'm okay to get up," she said, the rain starting to seep through her clothes. She moved her legs to make sure she hadn't twisted anything.

"Let me help you." Gabe bent over her and supported her shoulders and elbow as she tentatively stood up. "Okay, tell me if it hurts when you put your weight on it."

"I'll be fine," she insisted. She took a step forward but when she put her weight on her injured leg, she faltered and reached for Gabe's arm. She looked down and saw that the towel was blood-soaked and the rain was making the blood run down her leg in rivulets.

"Take this," Gabe ordered, handing her the driftwood.

Seconds later, he had scooped her up and was striding quickly to the path leading to his property. Her cheek brushed against his chest as he carried her up the slope to the path that led to the manicured lawn at the back of his house. After setting her down gently, he opened the door and she gingerly stepped inside.

He pulled a chair over to where she stood. "Have a seat and I'll grab some towels and tend to your cut."

Angel was about to say she could look after it herself if he could just supply her with a few bandages, but he was gone before she could open her mouth. She sighed.

She had no choice but to rely on Gabe. Again.

He returned with a face towel and a large bath towel that he placed over her shoulders. He waited until she had towel-dried her hair and arms, and then, kneeling by her chair, he removed his towel from her calf and proceeded to clean the area around the cut with cotton pads. "Sorry if this stings," he said, moistening a fresh pad with alcohol.

She winced, gritting her teeth as he gently dabbed the cut. He squeezed an antibiotic cream over the cut and then wrapped a strip of gauze around her calf.

"Okay, now to get you dry." He stood there looking at her quizzically. "Actually, I'm pretty wet now, too." He pulled off his hoodie, revealing a black T-shirt. "I'll grab you something you can wear while you dry your clothes. The dryer's in the next room." He strode across the room to a set of stairs.

Angel let out a pent-up sigh. What happened to the quiet day she had planned to spend at the B&B, reflecting on memories and processing Gramsy's loss? It seemed the more she wanted to be alone, the more the universe contrived to do the opposite, throwing her and Gabe together.

She glanced around at what was obviously the family room, with an oversize dark chocolate leather sectional and a couple of recliners, a live-edge coffee and side tables, and a sleek floor-to-ceiling fireplace with built-in bookshelves on either side. On one side of the room was a well-stocked bar area with leather stools and a mini kitchen. The room had been designed, like Gramsy's and other homes on this side of Chéticamp Island, to highlight the view of the waters of the Gulf of Saint Lawrence. A few magazines and newspapers were scattered on the coffee table along with a couple of hardcover books. The white wood walls and the steel elements around the high glass windows gave the room a cottage industrial look. Even with its masculine features, the room had a warm feel to it.

Ordinarily, Angel would be drawn to the bookshelves, being an avid reader and always curious about what others liked to read. But in wet clothes and with a gash on her leg, she wasn't about to move off the chair.

Gabe's footsteps drew her gaze back to the doorway where he reemerged with a plush cotton robe.

"Do you think you can manage throwing your wet clothes into the dryer?" He glanced at her leg. "If not, I can—"

"I can do it," Angel said crisply, reaching for the robe without looking at Gabe directly. "It shouldn't take long, and then I'll get out of your hair."

Gabe left the room and went upstairs, deciding to have a quick shower before changing. That should give Angel enough time to get her clothes dried. He'd drive her back to Gramsy's, as it was raining even harder, and even if it wasn't, he didn't think she'd want to walk the distance with her injured leg.

The hot shower felt good after being in wet clothes. As he shampooed his hair, his thoughts kept returning to Angel. She seemed hesitant around him, as if she didn't want to have to depend on him. Being an only child, like him, she was probably very independent and used to doing things and making decisions on her own.

Or maybe she was reluctant to be at ease with him until she met with him and the lawyer to find out how he figured in Gramsy's affairs. Perhaps she'd even be more wary once she found out that he had been privy to Gramsy's condition and she hadn't been.

Angel would be hurt, of course. And he couldn't blame her. But he hoped that she would be willing to listen to him explaining how and why Gramsy made the decisions she did, and why she had trusted *him* to be the one to talk to her, and be involved with the lawyer to settle Gramsy's affairs.

Gabe rinsed off and wrapped an oversize towel around his hips. He towel-dried his hair, then headed to his walk-in closet and chose a Cape Breton T-shirt and casual cargo pants to change into. Checking the time, he didn't think Angel's clothes would have dried yet, so he decided to head down to the kitchen and see what he could whip up for dinner.

Even though Angel had said that she would "get out of his hair" after drying her clothes, maybe she would consider staying for dinner. He scanned the contents of his fridge and pantry and wondered what Angel's food tastes were like, beyond sandwiches like the ones they had enjoyed at the Cabot Trail Diner. Did she like simple meals with basic ingredients, or did she have gourmet tastes? If she decided to stay, should he make a simple lemon pasta dish topped with sautéed mushrooms and shaved Parmigiano? Or chicken cordon bleu with roasted lemon rosemary potatoes and an arugula salad?

From the main kitchen at the opposite end of the house, Gabe heard the faint sound of the dryer door being open and shut a few moments later. The laundry room was at the far end of the main floor, next to the family room that they had first entered.

He shook his head. Chances were, she'd want to get out of his hair, not stay for dinner. He closed the fridge door and put on a kettle. *She might appreciate a cup of tea, though...*

When Gabe returned to the family room, Angel was standing by the fireplace, scanning the bookshelves. She turned when she heard his footsteps on the oak floor.

"Thanks for the use of your dryer," she said. "I left the robe on the hook behind the door."

"You're welcome. And no worries. I have a few more upstairs," he said, smiling. "How's your leg?"

"Sore, but I'll be fine. I should be getting back to Gramsy's."

The whistle of the teakettle drew both their glances to the kitchen. "I thought you might like a cup of tea?" Her brows lifted and she hesitated but he didn't move, his gaze locking with hers.

"Sure," she said finally. "Thanks."

CHAPTER SEVEN

"Here's to Gramsy!" Gabe lifted his mug.

Angel hesitated slightly before lifting her mug of tangerine lemon tea to clink it with his. She looked around as she sipped her tea. The kitchen was an eye-stopper, eclipsed only by the stunning view of the Gulf of Saint Lawrence from what had to be custom-built windows. A chef's kitchen, with its massive six-burner range and double oven, and oversize steel refrigerator. The gleaming pomegranate-colored cabinetry was stunning. She had never seen such a vibrant color in any kitchen decor. The white quartz island, with its waterfall edges, black farmhouse sink, built-in butcher block and six cushioned steel stools, was impossibly long, and Angel couldn't help imagining the intimate dinner parties Gabe must entertain, perhaps alongside a special lady.

She cut off those thoughts swiftly. She might as well take the opportunity to ask him some questions. She set down her mug and stared at it for a few moments before fixing him with a direct gaze. "Okay, Gabe, I need you to clarify a few things for me."

Gabe's brows lifted at the mention of his name. She was well aware that she hadn't used it before. The main reason she had avoided it was because it put them on a familiar level—like in the past—and she wasn't comfortable with that. And now, it had just slipped out.

"What would you like to know, Angel?" He gazed at her steadily.

He had no problem using her name.

"I was going to wait until we went to the lawyer's, but I'd like to get some things straight about Gramsy." She bit her lip. "I know you've been looking out for her since you moved back. Did you know that she had health issues? And if you did, why didn't you let me know? I'm sure Gramsy would have given you my contact number."

Gabe rubbed his chin. "She found out she had an irregular heartbeat about a year ago. She told me this a few months later, when she was finally scheduled to have an angiogram." He inhaled and exhaled deeply. "I encouraged her to tell you, Angel. More than once. And again when she had to undergo the procedure to get stents put in for the three blockages revealed by the tests." He shook his head. "But she started to get agitated and insisted that she didn't want to worry you while you were teaching, and that she'd let you know once you finished your courses and flew back here." He threw up his hands. "I didn't want to agitate her further. I drove her to the hospital, she had the procedure and stayed overnight, and then I drove her home the next day."

Angel blinked, trying to digest everything Gabe had said. "Did anyone else know? Bernadette didn't mention anything."

"No, I didn't tell anyone, and the only other person Gramsy told was her lawyer, when she went to…"

"Review her will?" Angel said softly.

Gabe nodded.

"She must have been worried about her health," Angel said, her heart twisting.

"I have to tell you, Angel, Gramsy never seemed worried about it. She was just worried about *you* and wanted to ensure that her affairs were in order. She actually met with her lawyer every year to review things, even before she found out about her irregular heartbeat."

Angel leaned forward to put her elbows on the table, and cupped her chin with both hands.

"She was so excited when you booked your flight, Angel. And up until two weeks ago, when I…when I found her, she was looking good, feeling good and in great spirits." He reached across to put a sympathetic hand on her arm. "She passed peacefully, on the swing your Grampsy made for her, looking out on the gulf."

Gabe's words and the image they evoked broke the dam building up inside her. As the tears started to stream down her cheeks, she rose from her chair and turned away. She heard Gabe's chair scrape the floor, and seconds later he was facing her.

"I'm so sorry, Angel," he said huskily, encircling her shoulders with one arm.

She found herself closing the circle and falling against him, not caring about their past, just needing a caring embrace at that moment. When both his arms tightened around her, she sobbed against his chest. Other than Bernadette, there was nobody on whom she could unload her grief, and she knew that there were many tears that were still pent up inside her.

When one of Gabe's hands reached up to cup the back of her head, Angel felt a surge of something familiar run through her. A feeling of being protected, cared for and cherished even, despite the fact that Gabe couldn't possibly feel those kinds of emotions for her now.

But he had in the past when they were young… at a local playground where a tourist had teased her—for losing her balance coming off a slide and falling flat on her face—before running off. She had burst into tears, feeling humiliated, and Gabe had rushed to her side, helping her up, gently brushing the sand and tears off her face and putting a protective arm around her to comfort her.

It didn't matter now. It was obvious that Gabe had cared for Gramsy in many ways, and Gramsy had trusted him implicitly, and that made her feel some kind of connection with him.

Sniffling, she moved her head off his chest. "Sorry for the deluge on your shirt," she said gruffly.

"Don't ever apologize for your tears, Angel. They have to come out. That's part of the grieving process."

She nodded and looked at him through her blurred vision. "Thanks for being there for Gramsy over the years. I really should get back now." She wiped her eyes. "And thanks for the tea."

"My pleasure."

The rain had diminished to a light drizzle. Gabe drove her back in the sleek silver Porsche that was parked next to his Range Rover. When he pulled into Gramsy's, Angel saw Bernadette at the front living room window. She could only imagine what was going through Bernadette's mind as she witnessed Gabe opening the door for Angel and offering his hand to help her.

Bernadette opened the front door before they did. She looked closely at Angel. "Is everything okay? Why are you limping?"

"I'll tell you inside," Angel said. At that moment, a Jeep pulled into the driveway behind Gabe's Porsche.

"It's Ross," Bernadette said, her face lighting up. "With pizza."

They watched as Ross climbed out of his Jeep with two large pizza boxes and a gift bag. "Everyone come in," Bernadette said. "I'll introduce you inside."

Ross smiled at Angel and Gabe and entered first, handing the pizzas to Bernadette. Gabe turned to Angel.

"I'll say goodbye, Angel. I want to talk with you about a few other things Gramsy shared with me, but it can wait until tomorrow." He gestured at his Porsche. "You'll have to tell Ross to kindly move his Jeep."

Bernadette reappeared and heard him. "There's plenty of pizza for all four of us. Come on, you guys. Let's eat it while it's hot."

Gabe glanced at Angel.

She snapped out of her thoughts. The least she could do was to invite him in. "Yes, of course. You're welcome to join us, Gabe."

Bernadette nodded and went back in.

"After you," Gabe said, gesturing with his hand.

Angel stepped forward, faltering at a sharp twinge in her calf.

Gabe immediately reached out to encircle her and prevent her from falling.

Angel felt another twinge, only this one was closer to her heart.

Bernadette introduced Ross to Angel and Gabe, and after Ross expressed his sympathies to Angel, Bernadette ordered him and Gabe to sit and chat in the living room while she had a word with Angel in the kitchen. From Bernadette's frown, Gabe could see that she was reacting to Angel telling her about her leg injury.

A few minutes later, Angel joined them in the living room, choosing to sit at a recliner. Bernadette brought out plates and the pizzas, and set them on the large rectangular coffee table between the two couches. She asked Ross to fill the glasses on the island with the wine he had brought.

"Cheers, everyone." Bernadette raised her glass. Everyone leaned forward to clink glasses with each other. "Let's toast to Gramsy."

Gabe caught Angel's gaze and held it. "To Gramsy." He wondered if this would incite fresh tears, but this time Angel just smiled briefly at him and nodded. When everyone had helped themselves to pizza, he reached for a couple of slices of the Pizza Bianca, with its "white" sauce of olive oil, cheese and fresh rosemary.

"Mmm, this is really good. Maybe I should consider opening another restaurant that just serves pizza," he chuckled.

"Do you remember the first time Gramsy let the three of us help her make pizzas?" Bernadette said, gazing from Gabe to Angel.

Gabe and Bernadette exchanged a look and then burst out laughing. They were both the same age, and Angel would have been seven and they ten at the time.

"Gramsy left us to join Gabe's parents and my grandma out on the back patio. Gabe started to brush the sauce onto the first pizza and I was in charge of the second pizza. *You*—" Bernadette pointed accusingly at Angel "—started sampling the ingredients, popping a mushroom into your mouth, and then a slice of pepperoni, and on and on."

"And when I told you to stop eating all the ingredients on the pizza, you took offense and decided to dab my face with the brush," Gabe said, smirking. "I called you a brat—teasingly, of course—then Gramsy came in and you played the innocent. Just like now."

Everyone laughed as Angel's mouth dropped and she crossed her arms, raising her chin in defiance. "I object to my childhood reputation being tarnished in such a manner." She sniffed and reached over to get the last piece of the Pizza Bianca at the same time he did.

"You can have it," Gabe told her, his lips twitching.

"Is that your way of finally making up for calling me a brat?" She took a bite and stared at him, her eyes narrowing.

Gabe couldn't help chuckling. "Okay, let's go with that." He picked up his glass of wine on the coffee table, and as he was swirling it, he could feel the relaxed vibes in the room. The shared memories and laughter had obviously helped set a lighter tone to the evening. It was good for Angel to have moments like this to help balance the more difficult and grief-filled occasions that were sure to arise.

For him, too.

The loss of Gramsy hit him at different times. She had truly been family to him. He hadn't had the chance to tell Angel how much Gramsy had meant to him, but he would when the time was right. When they were alone. Right now, the four of them were at ease with each other and with sharing a meal. The thought occurred to him to treat them to dinner at his place or his restaurant. He smiled, remembering something Gramsy had mentioned to him over the years: *I love my friends and cooking for them, and my friends can always feel that love in my cooking.* That love extended also to Gramsy's B&B guests, whom she treated like family.

The thought of family choked him up. Even though he had just met Ross and hadn't seen Angel for ten years, Gabe felt a closeness with the group. A familiarity, with Gramsy at the heart of it.

He looked up and realized he was alone in the room with Angel. Bernadette and Ross were in the kitchen, Ross leaning over the island while Bernadette made coffee. Angel was looking at him quizzically.

"I'm sorry," he said huskily. "My mind wandered off for a moment." He glanced at his watch. "I should probably head back home."

Bernadette heard him from the kitchen. "Oh no, not until you have dessert, Gabriel McKellar." She lifted up a tray. "I made these especially for Angel, even though it's nowhere near Christmas."

Gabe lifted his eyebrows. "Pork pies? How can I resist? One of Gramsy's specialties." They were one of his favorite traditional Cape Breton desserts that usually surprised tourists with their misnomer. Gramsy always made some for him during his summer visits, and of course at Christmas these past three years. It was rare for him to only have one or two of them. His mouth watered just at the thought of the buttery tarts with their filling of dates and brown sugar, and a creamy maple frosting on top.

"I'll make tea for anyone who wants it, Bernie," Angel said, getting up.

"You sit down, miss. Ross and I can handle it. Besides, you have a boo-boo. Sit down and relax."

Angel threw up her hands. "I'm not helpless," she protested. "I can still walk." She sat back down and shook her head at Gabe. "She's so bossy," she murmured.

"I heard that!" Bernadette called out.

"I love you," Angel returned with a grin. She gazed back at Gabe, and for a moment, her words seemed to linger in the air between them. Then she looked down and brushed something Gabe couldn't see off the couch.

A few moments later, they were all back in the living room, having tea or coffee and oohing and aahing over the pork pies. Ross was the first one to leave shortly after, explaining that he had an early meeting with another Realtor whose client was interested in a summer property on Cape Breton Island. Bernadette walked him to the front door and their murmurs and brief silence before the door clicked open seemed to intensify the awkward silence now between him and Angel.

Bernadette came back and gave them both a parting hug. "I have the early shift tomorrow," she said. "Try to get a good sleep, Angel. Bye, Gabe."

After she left, he turned to Angel. "Now that I've been fed and fortified, I think I'll call it a night, too."

Angel hesitated a moment before nodding and he couldn't help wondering, from the uncertainty in her gaze, if she wanted him to stay a bit longer.

Like he did.

CHAPTER EIGHT

ANGEL UNWRAPPED THE gauze bandage around her calf. The cut was no longer bleeding but she placed a fresh bandage over it before returning to her bedroom. She sat on the edge of her bed and pulled back the quilt and top sheet.

Tonight she didn't feel as bereft. Being with Bernadette and meeting the guy that was putting stars in her eyes had distracted Angel from the heaviness of her grief. Ross had been kind and attentive, and genuine, as far as Angel could see. He hadn't seemed like a stranger at all. Angel couldn't wait to tell Bernie how happy she was that they had found each other.

And what about Gabe?

In less than two days, she had experienced a flurry of emotions in his company. Irritation and confusion at their initial encounter, embarrassment at napping against him on the way to Gramsy's and a surge of grief and tears at the first sight of the house. This morning, surprise that Gabe made breakfast for her, and later, another wave of sadness and more tears, this time against his chest, for goodness' sake. And tonight, she even found herself laughing. The apprehension she'd felt at first at Gabe's joining them had dissipated as they sat around the coffee table, enjoying the pizza and easy banter.

There *were* a couple of times, though, when her and Gabe's gazes had locked, albeit briefly, that she had felt something aflutter in her chest. Something familiar. Something that came and went almost immediately. Had she imagined it?

Perhaps it was just a physical reaction to the way he looked. Those teal-green eyes were not hard to look at. And it was certainly not hard to listen to him talk, with his deep Scottish brogue. The way he rolled those *r*'s.

Angel couldn't help wondering if he had a woman in his life. Three years ago, Gramsy had been excited to share that Gabe was moving permanently to the family estate on Chéticamp Island. Months earlier, she had expressed her sadness over his parents' death, and how bad she felt for Gabe. They had been good friends over the years, and she would miss their summer visits.

Gramsy had also added that it was a pity that Gabe not only had to deal with the loss of his parents, but also with the breakup with his fiancée. It was just about the time she had broken it off with the guy she had been dating for three months.

She had met Colin Baxter at the high school where he taught drama, and was director of the *Beauty and the Beast* production the school was putting on for the elementary schools in the north end of the city. Angel's kindergarten students loved the performance and on their way out, she thanked "Mr. Baxter" and told him that she hoped the school would continue to do such wonderful plays. He shook her hand, thanking her for the feedback, and Angel felt that the handshake lasted much longer than it should have. When he finally let go of her hand, she smiled, feeling awkward, and quickly shepherded her children outside and back into the waiting bus.

A week later, Colin called her school during lunch and asked to speak with her. He asked Angel if she would be interested in meeting him. If she was, he would call her at the end of the school week. Angel hesitated at first and then said okay, trying to sound casual, but inside, her emotions were causing her heart to flutter and her cheeks to burn. She said nothing to her colleagues, though, reluctant to mix her personal life with her professional life.

The excitement of the anticipation of the first meeting and then the next, and the ones to follow, made the days and weeks pass quickly, with her and Colin getting together on either Friday or Saturday evenings for a date. As time went on, Angel wondered if he was going to introduce her to his parents. Missing her own parents, she was curious about Colin's family and mentioned it a few times to him. He promised Angel that she would eventually meet them, but something always seemed to come up to prevent this from happening.

The week before Christmas, on a Friday, Angel invited Colin for dinner at her apartment. She prepared a meal of his favorite foods: spaghetti and meatballs, Caesar salad and Key lime pie. Before dessert, he excused himself and while he was in the washroom, his cell phone dinged. On her way to get the pie, Angel happened to look down at his phone and froze when she saw the text: Are you going to be much later at school? Liam wants you to tuck him in.

She faltered, feeling as if she had just been punched in the stomach. She knew then why he kept procrastinating about meeting his parents.

When Colin came back to the table, Angel was still standing there.

"Is everything okay?" he said, coming over to kiss her on the cheek.

Angel stiffened and turned away. "You got a text," she managed to say before starting to gather up the dishes on the table. *And a wife and kid.*

He frowned and left her side to pick up his phone. Seconds later, he turned to her with a sigh. "Look Angel, I can explain..."

She glared at him. "Don't bother. Now I get why you didn't want me to meet your parents. I feel sorry for your wife and your son. They don't deserve a person like you." She put up a hand when he opened his mouth. "Get out of my house, Colin. *Now!* I'm sorry I ever trusted you. And don't even *think* about calling me again!" And when he grabbed his jacket and was walking to the door, she called out, "I can see why you're in drama. You know perfectly well how to be two-faced."

After he left, the first thing Angel did was to block him on her phone and then she sank down on her sofa and let the tears flow. She felt betrayed, manipulated, used. And *stupid*. She barely slept that night, tossing and reviewing their dates together, and berating herself for trusting him. For falling for his charm, his good looks and his consideration of her—and his—work obligations during the school week, suggesting that a Friday or Saturday evening would work best for them both.

Angel held honesty in the highest order in a relationship and he had failed miserably on that count. She shuddered at the thought of how long their relationship might have continued if she hadn't seen that text.

She spent Saturday in her pajamas, ignoring the dishes still on the table. When she opened the fridge and saw the pie she had made for Colin, she wished she had taken it out and flung it at him. Sighing, she put on her dressing gown and brought it to the elderly couple in the next apartment, their eyes lighting up when they saw it.

How could she have been fooled for three months? She'd wondered for days. Had she missed other signs?

Yes, she had. Colin had been enthusiastic about an investment that had yielded him thousands of dollars, and he had encouraged Angel to buy in. She should have been more prudent in vetting the company, but she was busy with report cards, and she had blindly trusted Colin with her money. She vowed never to be so gullible in the future.

The loss of her entire contribution still rankled.

By the following Saturday after breaking it off with Colin, Angel vowed not to spend any more tears over him, and to focus on her job and the kids she loved to teach. After Christmas, she decided that once the school year was over, she would pursue her goal of taking additional qualification courses to increase her teaching options. This kept her busy for the last three summers. No time for dating.

Happy when she had finally reached her goal and completed her last course, Angel booked her flight to Halifax and didn't waste any time letting Gramsy know. Her happiness was short-lived when Bernadette called to tell her the sad news of Gramsy's passing.

Angel got into bed. She shut her eyes and made herself think of good memories of Gramsy. Ones that would make her smile or laugh instead of crying. Thinking about Colin had brought back bad memories. She wanted to forget him and just think about her beloved Gramsy.

Except that somehow, each good memory that her mind called up included Gabe in the picture.

Gabe bent his head against the wind as he strode to his Porsche, the rush of the waves of the nearby gulf even more audible in the still of the night. He breathed in the crisp air, never tired of the sound or scent of the ocean, no matter the season.

Despite the sad fact of Gramsy's absence, he felt that the tone of the evening had been upbeat, with the sharing of funny memories and good food. He liked the sound of Angel's laugh, and the fact that she could join in with the teasing remarks. He wondered how things would be now if their lives hadn't gone in different directions ten years ago.

Gabe was glad Bernadette was there tonight. He had always liked Bernadette, and over the years, he thought of her as being like a sister. There was never any pretense with Bernie, and her spirited—and sometimes mischievous—ways, at least when they were younger, made him think of the tales his mother told him when he was young about the fabled Cape Breton fairies that lived in a *sitean*, a fairy hill, where they enjoyed music and dancing. It was Gramsy who had actually told him, that first summer he had visited, that the name of nearby Inverness was actually "The Fairy Hill."

Gabe envisioned Angel as a more guarded fairy, but one that showed her strong spirit when she needed to, like when he had shown up at the car rental office and she demanded to know if he was a lawyer. She had a tender and sensitive side, too, openly displaying her grief over the loss of Gramsy.

At home a couple of minutes later, Gabe went into his office and rifled through a few envelopes to retrieve the letter he had received from Gramsy's lawyer, requesting that he and Angel meet with him once she arrived. Gabe had confirmed the appointment for the day after next, thinking that Angel needed a couple of days to herself before dealing with Gramsy's legal affairs. The letter briefly outlined Gramsy's wishes: that the lawyer disclose them in the presence of Angel and Gabe, and that, a week or so later, a small reception in her memory be held at her B&B for her closest friends. The lawyer would provide more details at the meeting.

Gabe actually knew a little more than Angel did, simply because Gramsy hadn't wanted to distract Angel during her teaching and summer courses, talking about her will. He and Gramsy had become very close, especially in the last three years since he moved back to Chéticamp Island. Gramsy had told him often that he had always been like a grandson to her, that he had helped her in countless ways over the years and that his concern for her and his not-so-subtle checking up on her to see if she was okay had warmed her heart. She always looked forward to having tea with him in the afternoon before he headed to his restaurant, and she would inevitably serve him whatever she had made for the B&B guests, whether it be scones, muffins or a piece of pie.

And, of course, she'd always mention Angel, her eyes lighting up when she'd declare that she loved Angel to the moon and back. After Gramsy's stent procedure, she told Gabe that she was thinking about the future and what to do with her B&B after she passed, and she earnestly hoped that he and Angel would be on board with her wishes. And if they weren't, she said, laughing mischievously, she would have to enlist the help of the fairies over in "Fairy Hill" to get them to see it her way. Gabe felt a wave of sorrow grip him. Gramsy was the closest person to him besides his parents, and at moments like this, thinking about times they had spent together and the trust she had put in him, the grief he felt would resurface. His grief for his parents had been overwhelming, especially in the first year after their tragic passing, but in the last two years, it had been tempered by the love and caring Gramsy had shown to him. And now that she was gone, he felt her absence deeply. If he had felt like an orphan three years ago, he felt that same sentiment now.

Gabe strode across his room to the large bay window overlooking the waters of the gulf. This fresh grief brought back memories of how alone he felt when his fiancée left. Charlotte had been unable and unwilling to deal with his lingering sadness over his parents' senseless death. Since moving to the island, he'd had plenty of time and space to process their relationship, and to see the cracks that had been there from the beginning. He could understand that he had been partially responsible, having put up an emotional wall between him and Charlotte, sensing that she was incapable of truly understanding what he was going through, as she had never lost anyone in her family. He was willing to take the blame for that, but he didn't regret it, because it had allowed him to see that Charlotte lacked the empathy and compassion he needed at the time. She couldn't deal with his heartbreak and with having to give up their social activities to "dwell in this dark place" he'd found himself in.

It was a blow at first, and it felt like the world was crumbling around him. Hearing a few weeks later from his sous-chef that Charlotte was seeing someone anew, Gabe felt the yoke of guilt slide off his shoulders. She was not the right person for him, never had been, and even though it had taken a tragedy for him to see that, he was relieved that it was over.

Yawning, Gabe headed for his bed. He would give Angel a call tomorrow and arrange a time where they could talk. *Alone.* He needed to at least share with her what Gramsy had told him. She had a right to know, and then they would be on a level playing field going into the meeting with the lawyer.

Gabe felt the gulf breeze from his open window fanning his face and upper body. Breathing deeply, he closed his eyes and thought about Angel, most likely trying to get to sleep herself.

"Sweet dreams, Angel," he murmured. "I'll see you tomorrow."

CHAPTER NINE

Angel woke up to the sound of a text. She reached over to grab her phone and squinted at it. *Gabe*.

Good morning, Angel. I was wondering if you might want to take a drive around and see what's changed in the area. And...we can talk more about a few things before the meeting with the lawyer tomorrow.

Angel sat up and stared at the phone for a few moments.

Angel? Are you there?

Uh, yeah, sorry, I just woke up and...and I'm not fully functioning until I have my first coffee.

Oops, sorry to interrupt your sleep.

That's okay.

Can I call you instead of texting?

Um...okay.

Seconds later, she answered Gabe's call. "Hello again."

"Hi. I hope you don't mind me calling. I prefer to hear a human voice, either by phone or in person."

Angel's thoughts flew to the text she had seen on Colin's phone. "I agree, actually. Although a text can be very illuminating about a person."

"And subject to interpretation," Gabe said. "Communicating with someone face-to-face is always the best option, whenever possible. So, do you—"

"Sure," she said lightly. "You can come by in half an hour?"

"Will do. I'm just near the end of my jog. I'll be there after my shower."

"Um...okay. If I'm not ready, just let yourself in. And you might as well make me a coffee."

In the shower, Angel wondered what had gotten into her, taking such a sassy tone with Gabe. She liked his unchecked reaction: that deep laugh, and even though she couldn't see it, she imagined the look of surprise in his eyes. Knowing he was showering at the same time she was gave her a funny feeling. And why did she feel shivers of anticipation running through her under the hot shower spray? *Did Gabe feel some kind of anticipation, too?*

She rinsed the rose-scented lather off her body and stepped out onto the plush bath mat. She dried herself briskly with an oversize towel, replaced her leg bandage with a new one and then wrapped the towel around herself while drying her hair.

Afterward, Angel opened the bathroom door tentatively. The welcome scent of percolating coffee wafted up the stairs. *Just like when Gramsy was alive.* Somehow it made her feel that Gramsy would approve.

She inhaled deeply and then dashed into her room to get dressed. She decided on a pair of black jeans and a soft, sky blue pullover. She gave a last glance at herself in her dresser mirror, decided to add a touch of blue eye shadow and then, ignoring her unmade bed, headed downstairs.

Gabe looked up, the coffeepot in his hand. He continued to gaze at her while she descended and arrived in the kitchen, sitting at the island opposite him.

"Good timing, Angel." He smiled, pouring her a cup. "And good morning. Your cut is better, I hope?"

He had selected two mugs that Angel had

bought for Gramsy at a local pottery studio. Each was a swirl of blues and white, evoking for her the image of the waves of the gulf, tinged with the foam of whitecaps.

"Good morning," she said, "and yes, my leg's better." She took a sip of her coffee. "Thanks for indulging me. It always—"

"Seems to taste better when someone else makes it," he laughed. "Is that a not-so-subtle hint for me to indulge you with breakfast, too?"

Angel shook her head, feeling a warm rush in her cheeks. "Not at all. I wouldn't have such lofty expectations."

He raised an eyebrow.

"I'm happy with a coffee to get me going. And then, maybe in a bit, we can stop for brunch or lunch somewhere."

"Of course." Gabe's eyes crinkled as he smiled. "Gramsy mentioned once or twice that she always made sure you were well-fed, or else—"

"Or else what?" Angel frowned, crossing her arms.

That laugh. Again.

"'Or else your usual angelic temperament might change.' Her words, not mine," he said defensively, holding out his hands.

"Really!" Angel said imperiously, raising her

chin. "What else might dear Gramsy have told you about me?"

"Do you really want to know? And remember, I'm just the messenger."

"Spill!" she said sternly, narrowing her eyes.

Gabe sputtered as he was drinking his coffee. He swallowed quickly and struggled to keep a straight face.

"Who *are* you?" she demanded, trying to restrain herself from smiling. "And what kind of details would my beloved Gramsy disclose to you?"

Gabe hesitated as he stared at her, tapping a finger over his lips. "It's all good, I promise," he said finally, a gleam in his ocean eyes. "You're smart, you're beautiful, you're a good cook, you're a great teacher, you're kind, you're—"

"Enough!" Angel put up a hand. "I don't need to hear any more." She looked down at her coffee. "I'll finish this and then we can go."

Angel's cheeks had turned pink, reminding Gabe of Gramsy's summer peonies. They looked just as soft as the petals, too. She looked up suddenly and their gazes locked. She *was* beautiful, and from her reaction, he wondered if perhaps she wasn't used to hearing an avalanche of compliments. Or maybe it made her uncomfortable because *he* was saying the words.

Minutes later, they were passing the bluffs, the grasses mingled with white, pink and yellow wildflowers swaying in the wind. The Porsche's windows were down, and Angel was transfixed on the view, her hair flying up around her and the scent of her floral perfume tickling his nose.

They passed Chéticamp Island Beach and Gabe put on some relaxing classical music, sensing that Angel did not want to be distracted from the views as she reconnected with the island. As he drove along Chéticamp Island Road, he decided to take the Cabot Trail north. He never tired of the stunning views of the North Atlantic Ocean and the impossibly steep cliffs and woodland promontories on Cape Breton Island's northwest coast. Knowing that there was a chance of showers in the afternoon, he wanted Angel to enjoy the trail in its full splendor while the sun was out. He would suggest going to Inverness that evening.

When Angel rolled up her window a while later, he did the same. "This is God's country," she murmured. "I've missed it. The wind, the waves, the heights. *Everything.*"

From his occasional glances in her direction, he could see that she was enjoying not just the views, but the music, too. When Pachelbel's Canon in D came on, she paused from her sightseeing to smile at him. "One of my favorites," she said, before leaning back in her seat, occasionally closing her eyes and swaying gently to the melody.

As he headed toward Pleasant Bay, Gabe turned off at a lookout point. "I thought we could stop and enjoy the scenic view from here for a few minutes. Shall we?"

He stepped out and went around to open Angel's door.

"Thanks," she said and walked to the guardrail. "Absolutely breathtaking."

Gabe watched her as she scanned the sky—now streaked with white wisps—and the massive woodlands jutting into each other, with the Gulf of Saint Lawrence visible between their clefts. A bald eagle, with its distinctive white head, soared majestically across the sky in the distance. "Breathtaking indeed," he said as she turned and caught his gaze.

"This is so different from living in the city," she said. "So calm."

"Would you ever move here from Toronto?"

"I'd lose my seniority." She shrugged. "But I do recall a teacher on my staff moving to the west coast, and saying that she'd lose her seniority, but her experience would be recognized for salary purposes."

"Gramsy mentioned you taking extra courses

these past three summers. Was it to get your principal's designation?"

Angel laughed. "No, no, no. I *love* being in the classroom. I was taking additional qualification courses, namely, advanced French immersion in order to get my Certificate of Bilingualism. Which I *did*."

"Félicitations, Ange! Sois fière de toi-même."

Surprise flashed across her face at his "Congratulations, Angel. Be proud of yourself." *"Merci beaucoup,"* she replied with a smile. "Your French is good."

"I've learned a few select phrases since moving permanently to Chéticamp Island, with its French Acadian heritage," he chuckled. "I'm getting better. I should keep practicing, though."

"Mais, oui, monsieur," she said teasingly.

They both laughed, and the way Angel's eyes were sparkling in the sunlight made something catch in Gabe's chest. "Okay, let's continue on, *mademoiselle*. I don't know about you, but I'm thinking we should stop for a bite soon."

"Sounds good," Angel said. "I just want to take a couple of photos first."

Gabe nodded and opened her door before getting into the driver's seat. He smiled as he saw her taking a selfie against the backdrop of the highlands and gulf.

As he continued driving a few minutes later,

Gabe couldn't help thinking how remarkable it was that sadness and happiness could coexist. He and Angel were both grieving the loss of Gramsy in their own way; yet, they had managed to experience moments of happiness and beauty.

Together.

Being with Angel was so different from being with Charlotte. He hadn't observed any sign of an inflated ego, or a sense of entitlement. And he hadn't seen any evidence of snobbery or pretension, being from a big city. Angel was simply being herself, as she had always been in the past… "Oh, there's the Rusty Anchor!" Angel said, pointing. "My mouth is watering, just thinking about the food I had there with Bernadette the last time I was here, before doing the whale cruise tour."

"Lunch there, then?" Gabe laughed. "It'll be breakfast, too."

"Let's do it! I'm starving."

"I've never been disappointed with any of the restaurants I've been to on the island," Angel said. "The fish and chips are the best, wherever you go." She bit into a sweet potato fry. "Mmmmmm."

"I agree," Gabe said. He'd ordered the same, "Cape Breton Style Fish & Chips." "Since we're talking about delicious restaurant food, I'd like to invite you to my restaurant tonight."

"In Inverness?"

Gabe nodded, his lips twitching. "We can fly to my restaurant in Scotland another time." He looked around. They had arrived before lunch and although only a few tables were occupied, he knew that soon the restaurant would be filled with tourists dropped off by bus during their tour of the Cabot Trail. Now would be the best time to talk to Angel about Gramsy's wishes. "Coffee and dessert, Angel?"

"Oh yeah," she laughed. "I spotted strawberry shortcake on the menu."

"Perfect. I'll have the same."

After the waitress took their order, Gabe leaned forward. "Angel, are you okay with discussing Gramsy's wishes?"

Angel sighed. "I have no choice, really. Look, I know Gramsy trusted you as a friend and neighbor. And she really did think of you as a grandson, Gabe. So—" she gazed at him steadily "—I want to hear whatever you have to tell me."

"Okay. First of all, you are Gramsy's only heir, and so her entire estate, including the B&B, goes to you. She told me this about a year ago."

"But she didn't think it important enough to tell me," Angel murmured, frowning.

"She didn't want you to worry needlessly. And

she wanted to be proactive about her decisions. Decisions that would impact your life."

"Well, I'll have no choice but to sell the B&B," she said, her face slumping into her hands. "I can't just pick up and move to Cape Breton Island."

Gabe surveyed her for a few moments. "Would you sell it to me?"

CHAPTER TEN

"What? Really?" Angel blinked. "What would you do with it?"

"I can think of a few things. For one, I could keep it as a guesthouse for any out-of-town chefs in training for my restaurant in Inverness. Or I could keep it running as a B&B in honor of Gramsy, after hiring the right people to handle the various responsibilities."

Angel was stunned. "Wow. I don't know what to say."

"You don't have to say anything right now, Angel. I know it's a lot to take in. I just want you to know that you have options, and whatever you ultimately decide to do, I'm here to support you. And I'll be with you at the lawyer's, as per Gramsy's request."

Gabe's eyes held concern, as did his voice, and yet, Angel felt a sudden surge of anxiety. And pressure. It wasn't Gabe's fault; he was just presenting the reality of the situation. It was just too much to think about right now. The drive so far on the Cabot Trail had been a distraction, keeping her mind off her grief over Gramsy's passing, and subconsciously, it must have been a welcome coping mechanism. But like it or not, she had to accept that Gramsy was gone, and that these practical matters had to be dealt with. By *her*.

Something didn't sit right with her about the situation. She picked at her fries, unable to look at Gabe directly. He wanted the B&B. Is that why he had been so pleasant and accommodating with her? Perhaps he thought that if their friendship of the past were to resume, he could get a better deal when she sold it to him.

The memory of Colin swindling her gave her a sinking feeling in the pit of her stomach. Perhaps he hadn't even invested the money and used it for himself instead. He had shown up one evening wearing a Rolex watch, and although he said it was pre-owned, the price he paid must still have been exorbitant…

She couldn't be sure about him, and now she couldn't be sure about Gabe's motivations. How could she trust Gabe, anyway? On her sixteenth birthday, he had told her he had feelings for her after he had given her the shell and gold chain. She had believed him but the sweet promise of a relationship in the future faded after he returned to Scotland and she to Toronto.

Gabe finished his degree in business and then was accepted into a prestigious culinary academy, a dream he had always had. Angel pursued her dream of becoming a teacher. They exchanged emails for a while, both apologizing for the lapses of communication, but eventually those dwindled while they each fulfilled their passions.

And sadly, the spark they had felt on the beach never progressed to a flame. How could it, with the ocean between them, and Gabe not being able to return to the island for years? All she was left with were the memories of his kisses and his gift.

Angel inhaled and exhaled deeply. Gramsy had obviously trusted Gabe, but could she? In one way, she was dreading the meeting with the lawyer, simply because it would be one step closer to the limited time that she had on the island to deal with things before flying back to her life in Toronto.

She stifled a sob just as the waitress arrived with their coffees and strawberry shortcakes. The restaurant was suddenly swarming with a tour group chatting excitedly as they settled at a number of tables. Neither she nor Gabe talked while they ate, and after a few bites, Angel put down her fork. "I'll have to take this home."

Home. Funny that she would call it that. She

had never thought of it as *her* home. Yes, it had been her home away from home for a few weeks every summer since as far back as she could remember, but it was always Gramsy's home. And now it was her temporary home while she settled Gramsy's affairs.

Gabe called their waitress over to pay the bill.

As soon as they were both in the Porsche, Angel turned to Gabe. "Thanks for lunch and… for the drive. I'd like to go back to Gramsy's now." She wanted to be alone. Alone to think, to cry and to think some more about the future of the B&B without Gramsy. And without *her*.

Gabe raised an eyebrow and was about to say something, then just nodded.

After driving for about twenty minutes, he glanced briefly at Angel. "I'm sorry if I upset you, talking about the future of the B&B."

Angel bit her lip. "I know I have to face the reality of the situation. I just got overwhelmed."

"That's understandable, Angel," he said. "It's a lot to take in." He paused to concentrate on the road as a series of transport trucks zoomed by.

Angel studied Gabe's profile. He had a straight nose and strong jaw, his trim sideburns connecting with his sculpted beard. His mustache was impeccably trimmed above his lips. He was a man who obviously cared about his appearance.

And there must be plenty of women who cared about his appearance also.

"*Stop it*," she told herself, and when Gabe turned to her with raised eyebrows, she realized that she had actually spoken.

"Sorry," she blurted, feeling her cheeks burn. "I wasn't talking to you."

Gabe pulled over onto a side street and parked. "Angel, I think that we should postpone dinner at my restaurant. Save it until after the lawyer's meeting tomorrow, or another day. Why don't you take the rest of the day and evening to relax. We can talk tomorrow."

Angel met his steady, blue-green gaze. She didn't want to go out for dinner at Gabe's restaurant—at least, not tonight—but on the other hand, she wanted to know more about his interest in Gramsy's B&B. "I think we should postpone it, too. I would rather stay home and talk more there." She heard Gramsy's voice telling her on more than one occasion to give people the benefit of the doubt. She should at least hear Gabe out, listen to what he had to say with an open mind.

Gabe nodded. "Okay, then, Angel. How about I whip up something for dinner and we can talk more after that. Since my fridge and pantry are stocked, why don't you come over to my place?" His eyes crinkled at the corners as he smiled. "I make a mean lobster mac and cheese. It's one of my favorite comfort foods."

Angel blinked. Lobster mac and cheese was one of *her* favorite foods. In fact, Gramsy always made it for her on the first and last day of her yearly summer visit. *Had Gramsy shared this information with Gabe on one of his visits to her place for tea?* She eyed him suspiciously. "Did Gramsy tell you—"

Gabe laughed. "She did. But she also made it for me a few times when I was young, after I finished some chores or errands for her. And eventually, she showed me how to make it. I must have been twelve. Now I make it at least once or twice a month." He cocked his head at her. "What do you say? I can stop at Chéticamp Fisheries on the way home."

Angel's eyes widened. "My mouth is watering already. I'd be crazy to pass up a chance to have lobster mac and cheese. What can I bring?"

"Yourself and your appetite," he laughed. "Nothing else. Okay, that's settled. *Allons-y?*"

"*Oui*, let's go."

Gabe's smile lingered as he drove back onto the Cabot Trail and headed south to Chéticamp. "Mind if I put on some music again?"

"Not at all," Angel said. She settled back in her seat and closed her eyes as the mellow notes of a harp gently broke the silence. She had always loved the relaxing effects of Celtic music, and often listened to it while meditating or doing yoga exercises. And often, after returning from a hectic drive in rush-hour Toronto traffic, she unwound by running a hot bath with rose or lavender-scented Epsom salts, and listening to one of her favorite Celtic CDs. She found the harp melodies especially soothing, and when she couldn't sleep for nights after discovering Colin's duplicity, she played the tunes in a loop until finally succumbing to sleep.

Gabe's smooth driving, combined with the peaceful music, gave Angel a sense of calm, making the previous wave of overwhelm she had experienced begin to dissipate. As she felt the tension in her shoulders lighten, her eyes opened, connecting with Gabe's. He turned his attention quickly back to the highway, but not before Angel noticed the gentleness in his gaze.

A look that caused a warmth to spiral through her body and her heart to melt a bit, despite her intentions of staying on guard. Since Colin, she had kept her heart locked, frozen to any possibilities of a serious relationship. She closed her eyes again, hoping the heat in her cheeks wouldn't betray her feelings should he turn to look at her again.

What are your feelings? an inner voice whispered.

I like him.

Angel let out a long breath she had been holding in. Yeah, she liked him all right.

Gabe was glad Angel hadn't turned him down when he'd invited her to dinner at his house, although he would have understood if she had chosen to stay at Gramsy's, a place that held special meaning and memories for her. The fact that she wanted to talk more about the B&B was a good thing.

Her reaction at the restaurant had taken him aback at first, wondering if she had assumed the worst about his intentions. That he was trying to manipulate her in some way so that she would sell the B&B to him. He had felt a twinge of hurt, but with Angel's enthusiasm for his lobster dinner, his spirits had returned.

And he was more than happy to be able to cook for her. Cooking was his happy place, always had been. Sharing his culinary creations with others made him even happier. It was too bad that cooking for Charlotte hadn't quite given him the warm fuzzies he expected. She had preferred to dine in his restaurant rather than having him cook for her at his place. It had puzzled him at first, but as the months went by, he realized that she needed to be in public to be noticed, and to notice people noticing *her*. Being the girlfriend and then the fiancée of the Michelin-starred chef Gabriel McKellar looked good on her and she wanted to be seen with him at Maeve's, and out and about in general.

Gabe was not exactly a recluse, but socializing six days out of the week was a bit much. More than a bit much. He didn't like the pressure he was starting to feel with Charlotte expecting him to end his evenings at his restaurant with an alternating group of her friends, friends she had invited to dine there. Of course, he was grateful to her for recommending Maeve's to her associates, but after the intensity of working with his crew to prepare his signature dishes night after night to a clientele that expected the best, all he wanted to do was to go home and relax.

He glanced quickly at Angel. She seemed more relaxed now, her lips curved in a slight smile, her fingers moving with the harp strains. His gaze reverted to traffic, but the image of the soft curve of her lips kept breaking into his thoughts.

He forced himself to think about the dinner he'd be making. The only thing he needed to pick up was the lobster. The fresh-catch season was actually over, but customers could still obtain them from local distributors during the year, as the lobsters were kept in holding tanks. As a restaurateur, Gabe made lobster dishes that were renowned not only on Cape Breton Island, but throughout the Maritime Provinces. He was proud to support the local island fishermen who worked to ensure the ethical and sustainable practices of lobster harvesting.

His restaurant in Inverness was packed every evening except Sunday and Monday, when it was closed. There were many return customers whose preferences ranged from his lobster chowder, chili and rolls to his Gramsy-inspired lobster mac and cheese. He was proud to feature traditional island dishes but also experimented with new creations, using local products and plants, many of which were grown in his year-round temperature-controlled greenhouse situated on his restaurant property.

He'd have to bring Angel there for a tour.

He stopped himself. Why was he thinking of making any kinds of plans with Angel? She wasn't here for a tour or anything of that nature. She was here for one reason only: to see Gramsy's last wishes honored. And, as the lawyer would explain in more detail tomorrow, to have a simple gathering of close friends at the B&B. Gramsy had confided in him that when she was gone from this "island paradise," she wanted a plain and simple send-off in her own home. *With my darling Angel and some of your cooking, dear Gabe, and fiddle music, of course.*

Gabe smiled at the memory but at the same time,

he felt a prickle behind his eyelids. He was going to miss that funny, quirky, amazing, lovely, generous and affectionate woman who had become family to him. The best kind of family, with a heart as big as the hearth in her home.

He blinked hard and was relieved to see the Chéticamp Fisheries sign come into view. "We're here," he said briskly, and when Angel started, he apologized for his loud tone. "It doesn't exactly go with gentle harp music." He turned off the ignition. "Want to join me?"

Angel shook her head. "No, I'll just feel guilty seeing them in their tanks." She shrugged. "Better just to wait until you serve me your mac and cheese."

"Oh, *I'm* going to serve you, am I?" he teased.

She blinked, opened her mouth to say something and then just laughed. "Well, since Gramsy isn't here to spoil me with her famous cooking, and *you* are probably the only person she shared her recipe with, I'm sure she would expect you to carry on her tradition and—"

"And spoil you?" He stroked his beard thoughtfully. "Hmm. I'll have to give this some serious thought." He flashed her a smile and got out of the vehicle. When he looked back as he was opening the door to the building, Angel was still looking at him.

And yes, she was still smiling, too.

CHAPTER ELEVEN

ANGEL WATCHED AS the door closed behind Gabe. She immediately pulled down the car visor to look at herself in the mirror. Just as she thought. Her cheeks were flushed a cranberry red. *She* was the initial cause, she acknowledged, with the silly words that had popped out of her mouth. *Better just to wait until you serve me.*

And he had just flown with it. The teasing glint in those ocean eyes and the flash of his perfect teeth when he smiled had ignited something inside her that she hadn't felt with anybody. Not even Colin. She flipped back the visor and took a deep breath in and out, hoping the flush would subside by the time Gabe returned to the Porsche.

Mercifully, Gabe focused his attention on driving for the rest of the way back to Gramsy's.

"Dinner at six okay?" he said as she turned to get out of the car.

"Sure," she said, nodding. "Um, why don't

I bring dessert? I'm sure Gramsy's pantry is stocked."

His mouth twitched. "If you insist. Angel food cake, perhaps?"

Angel rolled her eyes. "Maybe devil's food cake would be more appropriate."

"Touché." He grinned. He glanced at the sky. "Looks like rain again. Shall I pick you up at five thirty?"

"Even if it does rain, I'm not made of sugar," Angel scoffed. "I'll walk over, thanks."

Gabe waited until Angel was inside before driving away. She checked the time and then the walk-in pantry. All the main baking ingredients were there, and when she peeked into the upright freezer in the pantry, her heart twinged to see all the containers and items Gramsy had made and labeled: half a dozen pie crusts, chili, seafood chowder, tea biscuits, blueberry scones, a variety of soups and breads and assorted meats, fish and seafood and poultry.

"Oh, Gramsy," she sighed, "I wish you were here with me." She closed the freezer door and walked to the built-in corner cabinet where Gramsy kept her various recipe binders.

All the binders would be precious keepsakes of Gramsy's legacy, her personal collection of tried-and-true recipes from over three decades. Angel wouldn't even think of returning home without them. She pulled out a pink binder labeled "Desserts" from the half dozen on the bottom shelf. Flipping through the pages of Gramsy's handwritten recipes, Angel stopped at one that caught her eye: butterscotch pie, and next to the title were the words *One of Gabe's favorites*. So the guy had a sweet tooth!

She scanned the list of ingredients and checked to see if she had all of them. *Okay, butterscotch pie it will be.* She returned to the freezer to take out one of the piecrusts and set it on the kitchen island before gathering all the ingredients for the filling and meringue.

It wouldn't take long to make, but it needed to cool down a couple of hours before serving. Which would take her close to the time that Gabe had indicated for dinner. *Perfect.*

Gabe was making a decadent lobster dish that *she* loved and she would be making and bringing over a decadent dessert that *he* loved.

Angel flipped through more of the binder and saw many of Gramsy's notations, including *her* favorites and ones that the B&B guests particularly liked. Next to the title *Chocolate Pudding Cake*, Gramsy had written *Angel and Gabe loved it!* And she had drawn a heart around their names, with the date.

Angel's heart drummed gently. She had been eight then. And Gabe eleven. She stared at the heart around their names. Angel was glad that Gabe had been close to Gramsy. Not just distance-wise, but emotionally. It comforted her to know that Gramsy had enjoyed teaching Gabe how to cook, and that he had shown his appreciation by naming his new restaurant after her.

And now he wanted to buy Gramsy's B&B.

Angie shook her head. Things were moving so fast, but she didn't want to think about it now. She flipped back to the butterscotch pie recipe. *Okay, Gramsy, let's hope I can make you proud...*

It wasn't as complicated as she first thought. She finished covering the pie with the meringue and slid it into the oven to bake for ten minutes.

Yes! It looked and smelled heavenly as she removed it and set it on the counter to cool. With a satisfied smile, she headed upstairs. She had plenty of time to have a shower or even a bath, and contemplate Gabe's query about selling the B&B to him.

It had never even occurred to her that he would be interested in buying Gramsy's place. And Bernadette hadn't mentioned anything of the kind, either. As Angel soaked in her lavender-scented bubble bath, she couldn't help feeling ambivalent about it. Selling it so quickly seemed somehow like a betrayal to Gramsy. *It should stay in the family.*

Angel sighed. Gabe *was* family for Gramsy. If *she* couldn't uproot and move to the island, then wouldn't selling it to Gabe make the most sense? She shivered and added more hot water so she could soak a while longer. Closing her eyes, she tried to imagine what it would be like to return to the island and *not* stay at Gramsy's. The property had been a part of her life for as long as she could remember. It would be bittersweet to leave it in someone else's hands. Even if it was Gabe.

And what if he followed through with keeping the place as a B&B? Who would run it? Cook and clean?

That's not your concern. But if he keeps it running, you'll have a place to return to.

Would she want to? Be a guest in a place that had been her home away from home?

Suddenly remembering that she had to refrigerate the butterscotch pie, Angel pulled the plug and stepped out of the bathtub. She tied her terry cloth robe around her and headed to the kitchen.

Moments later, when Angel was putting on the kettle for tea, the first fat plops of rain hit the kitchen window. The weather forecast of intermittent rain throughout the week was turning out to be true. She watched as it intensified. The views from this side of the house were so dramatic during a good storm. With her mug in hand, she walked to the living room and sipped her cranberry lemon tea while gazing at the waters of the gulf.

The rumbling of thunder and darkening skies leant a mysterious and romantic air to the place, Angel always thought, while the aroma of Gramsy's barley soup or crab cakes—or anything else, for that matter—permeated the whole house.

The memories that flooded her made her smile and at the same time brought a twinge of sorrow. There would be no more of Gramsy's cooking, no more treasured books, no more chats.

The sky seemed to darken even more at that moment, and when lightning flashed moments later in a stunning display, Angel knew the storm was about to get much worse. Again.

So much for walking over to Gabe's with the pie...

Gabe called Angel to tell her that he'd drive over to pick her up in a half hour. "I wouldn't want lightning to strike you or the dessert you've made," he said.

"I will graciously accept the ride," she said. "Unlike myself, my dessert *is* made of sugar."

He laughed. "Oh, I know at least one person who has referred to you as 'sweet.' In fact, I believe I heard her call you 'honey' a few times as well."

"Jeez, let me take a wild guess. Was it Gramsy?"

"You got it. And I think she was a pretty good judge of character," he added on a more serious note.

There was a long silence. "I better go and get ready, then," Angel said lightly.

"Okay, see you in two shakes of a lamb's tail."

He heard her laugh softly before hanging up.

Gabe strode into the kitchen to check the lobster mac and cheese casserole in the oven and then headed for the shower. He thought about how, in every exchange with Angel, something she said made him smile or laugh. He could still see the serious side of her, too, as serious as the eight-year-old who was determined to beat him in a race around the apple trees on Gramsy's property. She had some spunk in her, too. It was evident even when she was young, having the audacity to brush pizza sauce on his face.

After towel-drying his hair, Gabe changed into a pair of grey trousers and a light blue shirt. Casual and comfortable. Just like he hoped their dinner would be.

He checked the time, not wanting to keep Angel waiting. He put on an all-weather jacket and grabbed a golf umbrella in the entrance before dashing into his Porsche.

Moments later, he was at Angel's door under the oversize umbrella. Angel appeared in a bright yellow raincoat with a matching sou'wester hat and knee-high flower-designed rain boots. He couldn't help smiling, having seen Gramsy in that getup many times.

Angel's dessert was protected in a red plastic container that she was holding tightly. "Now you've captured my curiosity," he said, holding the car door open for her. "Can you give me a hint?"

"Hmm," she said, smirking. "Okay. Corn and liquor."

"Really? Let me think...a dessert made with corn and liquor?" He frowned. "I've been going through every dessert I can think of, and every dessert Gramsy made, and I'm coming up with *nada. Zilch.*" He turned into his driveway and turned off his Porsche's engine. He gazed at her quizzically. "Would you be so kind as to provide me with one more clue?"

Angel laughed. "Sure. Sea foam."

Gabe gazed at her for a moment. She looked so damn cute, grinning under that floppy hat. She looked like she belonged on the island. A true Acadian. He couldn't imagine Charlotte ever allowing herself to appear in anything so down-to-earth. If it wasn't recognizably designer, she steered clear away from it.

"Well? Have you figured it out?" Angel said, arching her eyebrows.

Gabe started. He had been staring at her. He wrinkled his nose. "I'm stumped."

A triumphant laugh. "All right, I guess I won't pick you as a partner on a game show. Okay, let's start with corn. Corn on the cob. What do you put on it?"

"Butter." Gabe narrowed his eyes. "Butter cookies! With rum!"

Angel made a harsh buzzer sound. "Not butter *cookies*."

Gabe stroked his beard. "Butter fudge?"

"No, silly. Think of a kind of liquor. *Your heritage.*"

"Butter...butter scotch? Butterscotch!"

"Butterscotch *what*?" She cocked her head imperiously at him. "'Sea foam' is my last clue."

Gabe tapped his lips with his index finger.

Angel feigned an impatient sigh. "What looks like sea foam on top of butterscotch—"

"Meringue!" he said triumphantly. "It's butterscotch pie, right?"

"Finally!" she returned, rolling her eyes.

He grinned. "I'm in heaven. You're an angel, Angel."

Angel shook her head and covered her face with her hands before spreading her fingers to look at him. "And you're a goof," she said, and climbed out of the car.

Gabe laughed and followed her to the front

door, not bothering to open up his umbrella. He'd have to change, but he didn't care. The rain was refreshing and the exchange he just had with Angel had felt so easygoing and *natural*. Her teasing had charmed him. Captivated him, as if time had stopped in the world around them so they could have these lighthearted moments together.

As they stepped inside his house, Gabe wondered if Angel felt the same. He caught his reflection in the large foyer mirror and his lips twitched. His hair was plastered on his forehead and rivulets were running down his cheeks. Was it his imagination, or were his eyes unusually bright? And his senses were tingling in a way that he had never felt before. Including the sense that Angel was gazing at him curiously. "I'll take your rain gear," he said, holding out his hand.

She set down the dessert container on the foyer side table and handed him her raincoat and hat. She had dressed casually, too, with a pair of burgundy pants and a white cotton blouse with flared sleeves. He smiled at the sight of her multicolored polka-dotted socks.

Angel caught his gaze. "One of my junior kindergarten students gave them to me as a gift on the last day of school," she said brightly. "A little girl called Tessa. Her father said she saw them at the dollar store and wanted to get them for me."

She laughed. "She chose seven pairs to last me the week. By the way, Mr. McKellar, I'm getting hungry and you're a wet mess."

Gabe glanced at the mirror. "I am, aren't I? I'll just go up and change," he said. "In two—"

"Shakes of a lobster's tail."

He burst out laughing. "Good one, Angel. Okay, make yourself at home. I'll be back in a few minutes to check the mac and cheese. Oh, and go ahead and put your 'corn liquor sea foam' creation in the fridge. By the way… It's one of my favorite desserts." Grinning, he leaped up the stairs two at a time.

CHAPTER TWELVE

Angel watched Gabe practically fly up the curving staircase, his hair and pant legs soaked. She shook her head and proceeded to saunter through the elegant foyer and spacious living area that connected to the kitchen and formal dining room. Angel breathed in the mouthwatering scent of the lobster mac and cheese and hurried to place her dessert in the fridge. Moving into the dining room, Angel saw that Gabe had set the table. A bottle of wine was chilling next to two goblets, and the elegant gold-rimmed tableware was a perfect match with the rest of the decor.

With nothing to do but wait for Gabe to return, Angel sauntered back to the living room and sat at one of the couches. She picked up a magazine on the coffee table and casually flipped through the pages until the heading of one article and the opposite page caught her attention.

"Michelin-Starred Chef Opens Mara's in Inverness."

She went on to read how Gabe had decided to return to Chéticamp permanently after losing his parents, and how his new restaurant paid homage to the French and Acadian history and culture, and featured his take on the traditional dishes of the area. The opposite page showed Gabe in his chef's hat and jacket, standing behind a table showcasing a number of his featured seafood and local dishes. The article explained how some of the dishes had their origins with the Indigenous Mi'kmaq peoples. She read on, and when she came to the paragraph explaining his decision to name his restaurant after Gramsy, Angel felt her eyelids prickle.

Everything came back to Gramsy.

Hearing Gabe's footsteps on the stairway, she hurriedly wiped her eyes and set down the magazine.

"I hope you're hungry," Gabe said, smiling as he joined her. His gaze flew briefly to the magazine before returning to her.

Angel nodded. "I almost started without you. That would have left you only with the butterscotch pie."

He laughed. "I should know by now to expect the unexpected to come out of your mouth. Now, let's head to the dining room so I can get some food into you."

Angel's gaze swept over him as he walked

away. He had changed into black linen pants and a teal shirt with sleeves rolled up mid-arm. His hair was slightly damp, curling at his nape, and his eyes, matching his shirt, made her pulse quicken.

She followed him in, and moments later Gabe had poured the Chardonnay and they clinked glasses. "To Gramsy," he said huskily. He drank and set down his goblet. He gestured at her steaming plate. "Enjoy."

Angel savored her first mouthful and sighed. "I have missed this." She had a few more forkfuls and then paused to sip her white wine. Its delicate, citrusy tones paired perfectly with the creamy lobster meat, cheese and corkscrew-shaped pasta. "I'm sure Gramsy is smiling, wherever she is." She dabbed at her lips with her napkin. "Thank you, Gabe."

"My pleasure. There will be plenty left over for you to take home."

"Maybe," she said slyly. "Maybe not."

Another deep laugh.

"I can see now why Gramsy said she never had to worry about food going to waste while *you* were visiting."

Angel shrugged. "Her fault for making such delicious meals. And now I'll have to start making her recipes on my own," she added wistfully.

"I'll need another suitcase to bring home all her recipe binders."

Gabe gazed at her for a moment. "Unless you reconsider and relocate *here*."

Angel finished swallowing another delicious forkful. "I can't see that happening. I have my job, my apartment, my friends…*everything* in Toronto. I don't really have a choice."

Gabe's brows furrowed. "Couldn't you get a teaching job here? Make new friends and have your friends from Toronto visit? From what I've experienced the couple of times I've been in Toronto, it's a pretty fast-paced existence."

"I'm used to it. Kind of," she said, her mouth twitching. "I'm north of the city. Downtown is another matter."

Gabe refilled her wineglass.

"Don't get me wrong," she sighed. "Living here would be a dream. I'll have to consider it when I retire."

"So you're fine with selling the B&B?"

Angel put down her fork. "Like I said, I don't have a choice." She gave Gabe a measured glance. "I thought about it more once I got home after lunch today. If I have to sell it to anyone, I might as well sell it to *you*. I'm sure Gramsy would approve."

"You don't think she'd prefer it if *you* stayed?"

Angel blinked. "Oh, of course. But it wouldn't

be the same without her." She took a sip of her wine and looked up to see a sheen in Gabe's eyes.

"You're right," he said softly. "It won't be the same without her."

Angel felt a twinge in her heart. Up until now, she had only really thought about her own grief at losing Gramsy. But it was obvious that Gabe felt just as bereft without the woman who had been a grandmother to him. It hit her that they were united in their grief and she felt a sudden urge to comfort him. "I'm sorry for your loss of Gramsy, Gabe. She loved you."

Gramsy had never kept her feelings for Gabe a secret, and since his move to Chéticamp, those feelings had become stronger. Angel noticed Gabe's Adam's apple bobbing and he cleared his throat, visibly moved.

"And I, her," he said gruffly. He stood up. "Shall we move to the living room for dessert? I'll grab the pie."

Angel nodded and pulled back her chair. As she entered the living room, she turned to see Gabe pressing his fingers to his eyes before grabbing the oven dish with the remaining mac and cheese. His gesture of emotion made a rush of warmth spread across her chest. At the same time, it somehow made her want to cry.

She felt a twinge of guilt. Perhaps she had misjudged him and his intentions.

A couple of minutes later, Gabe entered with her pie, two plates and forks, and a pie server. He cut a generous wedge for both of them and then sat down next to her before taking his first generous forkful.

"This. Is. Amazing." He sighed and gazed at her appreciatively. "I'm in heaven." He proceeded to dig in again. "You're not taking home any pie leftovers," he said, his gaze both teasing and challenging.

She burst out laughing. "Go crazy, Gabe. Have it for breakfast."

"If there's any left by then," he said. "I might just help myself to a midnight snack."

Her lips twitched. He was like a little kid wanting to raid the fridge while everyone was sleeping. Only there was nobody else who was sleeping in the house with him. At least not regularly, as far as she knew. And he wasn't a kid. She pictured him getting out of bed, hair tousled and just wearing boxers, and heading to the fridge. "Wh-at? Sorry?" She started, her cheeks burning as she realized she had been daydreaming.

"I said, Angel, that the rain has stopped and the sun is breaking through the clouds. Feel like going for a walk on the beach to work off some calories? Not that you need to work anything off," he added quickly.

Angel wondered if it was wise to say yes. Did she want to be walking side by side with someone who had managed to pull on her heartstrings several times tonight? Just his suggestion now had made her pulse quicken. *Again.*

She really should say no, thanks and just go home. She could walk back. But as Angel met his gaze, something in those mesmerizing green depths made her knees feel weak. "Sure," she blurted before she could stop herself. And she said it a little too breathlessly for her own liking.

"I'll just put the leftovers in the fridge and take care of the dishes later," he said. "Let's go before the sun disappears. Get your stuff and we'll go out back."

A few minutes later, they were on the beach. The gulf waters were still active, cresting and collapsing, but the breeze was warm. He breathed in its salty scent and glanced at Angel, who was absorbed in scanning the beach in front of her for shells or stones washed up by the surf. He couldn't help smiling at the picture she made, wearing Gramsy's raincoat and boots. She had brought her sou'wester again, just in case. It dangled from her hand as she walked, her gaze intent on the beach sand. Occasionally, she bent down to pick up a shell, rinsing it at the edge of the surf before shaking it and putting it in her raincoat pocket. It was just like the collecting they had done in the past. Suddenly she shrieked as the surf rushed up her boots, and she tried to step out of it but the force of the waves knocked her back. He lunged forward to prevent her from falling, and as she fell against him, he circled her waist with his arms and held her firmly while the surf receded. The new and spicy scent of Angel's perfume wafted up to him with the breeze as strands of her hair brushed his jaw. For a few seconds, he felt a sensation that he hadn't felt for a long, long time. *Desire.* His heart pounded as she turned to regain her footing and he pulled her even closer.

Angel looked up at him breathlessly and the memory of their kiss on the beach on her sixteenth birthday came back to him, accompanied by a piercing regret that he had let his studies and ambition for culinary school take precedence in his life once he'd returned to Scotland. They were an ocean apart, and the fledgling communication they had initially with each other had eventually ceased.

Was Angel thinking about that time on the beach? The kisses that had kept him up that night? Looking at her intense brown eyes now, he wanted nothing more than to taste her kisses again. The sound of the incoming surf broke into his thoughts and they both leaped away from the water's edge to avoid the surge.

They continued walking silently, the sky darkening as clouds shifted to block the sun. Along with the rushing surf were the intermittent cries of seagulls and the warbling sounds of roosting cormorants. Gabe could kick himself that he had missed his chance with Angel long ago and he knew it was unrealistic to think that they could recapture those moments and start over. She would be leaving soon, and both their lives would go on, just like before. There was no denying his attraction for Angel, but he couldn't start something that would just be coming to an end shortly. The back of Angel's hand brushed his momentarily, and he had to stop himself from taking her hand in his. He jerked his hand away and felt like a heel when she caught his reaction.

"I better be getting back," she said abruptly. "But don't let me stop you if you want to keep working off those calories."

Gabe cursed silently, hoping she didn't think he had recoiled at her touch. "No, I'll head back, too. The lawyer's meeting is bright and early. I'll pick you up at eight thirty."

Angel kept a wider distance between them as they walked back. The wind had picked up and she put on her sou'wester and hurried ahead, her shoulders hunched. When they arrived at his place, Gabe asked her to wait for a moment while he grabbed his keys. "I was just kidding about keeping the rest of the butterscotch pie," he said. "I'll pack it up for you."

Angel put up her hand. "No, it's all yours. And no need to drive me, since it's not raining, and my leg is fine. Good night." She gave him a half smile before walking away. "Oh, and thanks for a great meal," she called out without turning to face him.

He *had* offended her. *Damn!* He watched her as she disappeared from view. It would be awkward if he tried to catch up to Angel and apologize. What would he say? That he had moved his hand away from hers simply because he actually *wanted* to hold her hand? Uh, no. It sounded ridiculous and inappropriate. She probably had enough on her mind with the upcoming lawyer's meeting. He didn't need or want to complicate things for her. There was no use even hinting to her about his feelings when she had been very clear that she would be returning to Toronto—

He shut those thoughts down and turned to go inside. He hoped that Angel would sleep well tonight, although he wasn't so sure *he* would.

CHAPTER THIRTEEN

ANGEL GLANCED SIDEWAYS at Gabe as he drove. He had arrived at her door at precisely 8:30 a.m. She offered him coffee, but he politely declined, saying he had been up since five and had had his fill. He had shadows under his eyes and seemed less relaxed than previously, although he still opened the car door for her and made small talk about the weather.

"I hope you slept well?" He turned to gaze at her and she blinked in embarrassment.

"Uh, not bad," she lied. She had tossed, turned and tossed some more throughout the night, her thoughts alternating from the lawyer's appointment to the evening with Gabe. The dinner had been pleasant, the food delicious, but the way he had jerked his hand away from hers when they accidentally touched while walking on the beach left her with a strange feeling in her stomach.

She didn't know what to think. *He* was the one who had suggested they go for a walk. Was it normal for him to have that kind of reaction from his hand simply brushing against hers? She had been feeling mellow from the two glasses of wine she had enjoyed, one more than her usual, and when Gabe prevented her from falling and steadied her with his strong arms, she had felt lightheaded and her heart started beating erratically as his breath fanned her neck and the side of her face. She had almost wanted the moment to last longer.

Almost? an inner voice prompted.

Okay, so I was having a physical reaction to a guy who's freaking gorgeous and whose mouth was inches away from mine. That's perfectly normal.

Angel felt her cheeks burn. She pressed the lever to roll down the window and breathed in deeply.

"I can turn on the air-conditioning if you'd like," Gabe said.

"That's okay. I'd much rather the fresh Maritime air."

"Enjoy it while you can," he said, a husky edge to his voice.

"I wish I could bottle it up and take it with me," she sighed. "Along with some other things I love about this place…"

"Hmm," he said. "It will never leave you, even if you do go back."

If. Gabe hadn't said *when*. Was he thinking

or even hoping that she would change her mind about relocating?

With a sinking feeling in the pit of her stomach, she drank in the views as Gabe drove, wanting to store them forever in her memory.

"Well, here we are, Angel. You'll like Tom. He's easygoing, honest, professional and will help in any way he can."

Moments later, Gabe introduced her to Thomas Applebee and she shook his hand warmly. "It's nice to meet you, Thomas, even under the circumstances."

"Please. Call me Tom, although your dear Gramsy insisted on calling me Tommy." He chuckled. "She was the only one I let get away with it." His smile faded. "I'm so sorry for your loss, Angel. We're all going to miss her." He gestured for her and Gabe to sit in the plush chairs opposite his large mahogany desk. His office was in a historic building that also housed a store featuring Acadian antiquities and a collection of artisanal Chéticamp hooked rugs.

Angel nodded. "Thank you. And thanks for all you did to help Gramsy with her legal affairs."

Tom gave her a grateful smile. "That's very kind of you. She did reward me generously with one of her delicious pies or loaves whenever we met." His mouth turned down. "She spoiled me."

"As she did all of us," Gabe said, nodding.

Tom opened up a portfolio and took out a document. "As you know in the letter I sent to both of you, Gramsy wanted you both at the reading of her will. If there's anything you want me to clarify as I go on, please let me know."

Tom waited until they both nodded and then pushed up his glasses before proceeding with reading the clauses slowly.

As Angel was Gramsy's sole living relative, she would inherit Gramsy's estate, with several expectations: that a donation be made every year to the cultural museum to keep the Acadian culture in the area alive; that a scholarship in her name be handed out by Gabe yearly at the Culinary Institute of Canada in Charlottetown; and that a reception for her be held at the B&B for her close friends and neighbors after the legalities of her estate were finalized.

Tom looked up from the document. "Gramsy wanted some time to go by before friends gathered. She wanted the mood to be celebratory and, quote, 'not a downer.'" He smiled but his eyes were sad. "She requested that you and Gabe receive friends informally at the B&B and not in a stuffy room at a funeral home. Friends could drop in and share memories and enjoy fiddle music and Gabe's cooking."

Angel wanted to cry and laugh at the same

time. "I guess it's just as well that Gabe is in charge of the food," she said, her mouth twitching.

Gabe turned to her. "Hey, you can make the pie you made for us last night. Gramsy would love that."

Tom glanced from Gabe to her, his brows lifting.

"Um, I guess," Angel said, feeling the heat in her cheeks. She braced herself to ask Tom a question that had been niggling at the back of her mind. "In the letter you sent a couple of weeks ago, you said that Gramsy had wanted to proceed with...with the—" She choked up.

"With the cremation immediately," Tom finished sympathetically. "Those were her wishes, Angel." He reached out to put a comforting hand on her arm. "She wanted to make things as easy for you as possible." He glanced at Gabe. "And she had Gabe order an urn that she picked out herself online."

Angel met Gabe's gaze through blurred vision. "Gramsy was more forward-thinking than I thought."

Gabe held out the box of tissues on Tom's desk. "She sure was," he said gruffly.

"She ran the B&B with spreadsheets and had faithful followers on social media." He exchanged glances with Tom and then Tom said quietly, "I'll bring the urn to the B&B when you have the reception in her memory…"

At this point, Angel couldn't control the tears from spilling over her cheeks. She grabbed a few more tissues and wiped her eyes and face.

"Is there anything more, Tom?" she said, taking a deep breath.

"Yes, one more very important thing." He flipped a couple of pages before looking up. "Gramsy was aware that your life is in Toronto. She always dreamed that one day you might want to consider moving to Cape Breton Island and, specifically, Chéticamp Island. So, although she bequeathed you the B&B, she stipulated that, should you decide to sell it, that you give Gabe McKellar the first right of refusal, since she considered him family."

He paused, glancing from her to Gabe, letting them process the information.

"Okay, now here's what Gramsy added more recently. Knowing that you would certainly return to Toronto after the service, Angel, she would like you to rent it to Gabe for a year—if he's willing—while you have the year to think about it. That way, he can see if it will work out for him to buy it in the future, and you will have time before you make a permanent decision." He cleared his throat. "Gramsy didn't provide details, but simply said that the rent would help make up for a financial setback you unfortunately experienced a few years ago."

Angel felt her cheeks burn. She had told Gramsy about her failed investment with Colin. She took a deep breath. Would she be okay with Gabe potentially running the B&B for a year? She would have to be very clear about him upholding Gramsy's expectations on running the place. In any case, this arrangement would give her some breathing space and time to ultimately make a final decision. But would Gabe be willing to give it a go?

Tom tapped his pen against the document. "She said, and I quote, 'I love them both and I have every confidence that my Angel and Gabe will figure it all out.'"

Angel squeezed her eyes shut to prevent more tears from flowing. "This is a lot to think about. Do I…we have to decide and sign now?"

"No, of course not, Angel. Take your time." He handed her a business card. "Call or text when you're ready. Or if you have any other questions."

She nodded and stood up. "Thanks, Tom." She shook his hand and gave him a grateful smile. "I'll do that."

Gabe turned to Angel as she was putting on her seat belt. "Is there anywhere you need to go before heading back to the B&B? I'd be happy to drive you."

Angel's brows lifted. She checked the time on her phone. "Actually, I wouldn't mind if you dropped me off at Making Waves. Bernadette texted me this morning to meet her there for lunch. It's still a bit too early for that, but I can always grab a coffee while I'm waiting for her to go on her break. I have to think about everything Tom said." She turned away to gaze out her window.

"Sure." He drove out of the parking lot. "Angel, do you want to talk about the B&B? Just to clarify something... I had no idea that Gramsy would make that request of you."

Angel swiveled in her seat. "I think Gramsy meant well, but I think it just makes everything more complicated." She threw up her hands. "I just don't know what to do. I thought I would sell, and I would be fine with selling to *you*, but do I want to wait a year before things are settled? I'll be heading back to Toronto in less than two weeks."

Gabe pursed his lips. Angel really wanted to sell and be gone. *No strings attached.* He felt a twinge in his stomach. He, too, was puzzled as to Gramsy's conviction that he and Angel would "figure it out."

"I want to go back in a day or two to see exactly how Gramsy worded things in the will," Angel said decisively. "I'm sure there's an escape clause, or whatever you call it, so we don't have to wait a year to finalize things." With a hopeful smile, she leaned back and relaxed in her seat.

Moments later, the stylized sign bearing the words *Making Waves* appeared and Gabe turned into the restaurant parking lot. He had barely come to a stop and Angel already had her seat belt off. "Thanks for the ride," she said as she let herself out of the Porsche. She closed the door before he could reply and walked briskly toward the restaurant.

Gabe had hoped Angel would invite him to join her, at least for the time that she'd be waiting for Bernadette to get off for lunch. They could have talked more about Gramsy's wishes.

A couple of young adults walked by Gabe's silver Porsche and gave him a thumbs-up in admiration. He smiled and nodded and moments later drove out of the parking lot. It had been on the tip of his tongue to ask Angel if she'd like a ride back home, but she obviously had worked out something with Bernadette. It was early, but he decided he might as well head to his restaurant in Inverness.

The parking lot was empty when he arrived, but in a half hour or so, guests would be hard-pressed to find a vacant spot. Mara's was as popular at lunchtime as it was in the evening. He let himself in and grinned at the surprised looks from his sous-chef and staff when he strode into the kitchen.

"You can't stay away, eh, McKellar?" Chris Fox said teasingly as they moved into the dining room. Gabe had hand-picked him as sous-chef for Mara's after dining in a restaurant in Montreal where the young chef was getting acclaim for his traditional yet innovative dishes. After chatting with him several times and discovering that Chris was from Cape Breton, Gabe made him an offer to join him at Mara's. Chris jumped at the chance to return to the island, and since his return, had reunited with a high school girlfriend and married a year later. Customers had nothing but great things to say about him, and Gabe was grateful that their culinary paths had crossed and that now they were good friends to boot.

"You know I love you, Foxy," Gabe laughed. "Actually, I had business in Chéticamp and I thought I'd stop in for lunch."

"Well, make yourself at home." Chris smiled and glanced at his watch. "We open in exactly twenty-five minutes. Can I get you a coffee in the meantime?"

"No rush. I have things to mull over."

Chris eyed him closely. "Hmm. You sound serious. Does this by any chance have to do with the B&B and Gramsy's granddaughter?"

"You're a smart cookie, Foxy," Gabe said, shaking his head. "We'll chat about it another time."

Chris gave a mock salute and nodded, "Okay, boss. I better get back to the kitchen before the staff revolts."

Gabe strode over to a booth and slid to the spot near the window overlooking the seaside dunes and North Atlantic Ocean. The waves resembled flowing ribbons of blue-and-green silk along an endless golden beach. He never tired of taking in the panoramic beauty of this and countless other scenic spots on Cape Breton Island. He couldn't imagine any other place he'd want to live in.

Gabe shifted his gaze to the dining room with its gleaming mahogany bar and tables and plush tartan-upholstered booths. Large prints of scenic locations in the Highlands captured during various seasons graced the walls. His gaze rested on one scene of the Cabot Trail that reminded Gabe of the spot where he had stopped with Angel before stopping for lunch at the Rusty Anchor. The memory of Angel gazing in wonder at the view of the sweeping Highlands with the ocean backdrop caused a twinge in his chest. The sensation of knowing that she was as moved by the panorama as he was had somehow made him feel closer to her.

One of the scenes showed the Highlands in their brilliant autumn colors, the melding of red, orange and yellow resembling a rich carpet or quilt. People came from all over the world to see the stunning views of the Cabot Trail and Highlands throughout the year, but the epic autumn views were especially sought out.

He started as a waiter approached with a mug of coffee. "Thanks, Jeremy," he said, flashing a smile.

"Can I bring you a menu?" Jeremy said, his eyes twinkling.

"If I don't know my menu by heart by now, we're in trouble," Gabe laughed. "I'll wait for the official opening and just have a bowl of chowder and a couple of biscuits, and then I'll disappear until I'm back for my shift."

After Jeremy left, Gabe checked his phone. No messages. What was he expecting? A note from Angel? He inhaled and exhaled deeply. Why was he thinking about her so much? He took a drink of his coffee and then stared out the window again.

You don't want her to leave.

Gabe blinked. This random thought shook him. No, he *didn't* want Angel to leave. There was something about her, something familiar yet undiscovered, that was tugging at him like an invisible magnet. They had popped back into each other's lives again after ten years, their link being Gramsy and her property, of course, but now, with Gramsy gone, they both had only their memories, and the property.

Gabe started at the sound of people entering the restaurant. His thoughts were interrupted by approaching footsteps. He turned, expecting Chris or Jeremy with his seafood chowder, but the person a few feet away was the last person in the world he expected to see.

Charlotte, his ex-fiancée.

"Hi, Gabe," she said with a tentative smile. "I was hoping I'd catch you here…"

CHAPTER FOURTEEN

BY THE TIME Angel finished her cup of coffee, Bernadette had completed her morning shift. She set down the menu and gave Angel a warm hug before sitting across from her. "What do you feel like ordering, breakfast or lunch?"

Angel scanned both sides of the menu. "Hmm, let me see. What do you recommend?"

Bernadette laughed. "Everything! I'm surprised I haven't gained fifty pounds since I started working here!"

While they enjoyed Bernie's favorites—lobster roll and blueberry grunt—Angel filled her in on the meeting with the lawyer.

"Why would Gramsy want to make things more complicated?" she finished plaintively.

Bernadette shrugged. "I guess she wanted to give you a chance—and time, Angel—to consider making such a big decision in your life. And obviously, she trusted Gabe to look after the place until you ultimately decide. It's a win-win for both of you, really."

"But I don't have to wait a year to make up my mind. Much as I'd love to live here—who wouldn't? —relocating is not a viable option." Angel shook her head. "I don't know. I guess I'll have to just bide my time until the year has passed."

"It will fly by, Angel. Why don't you come back for a visit during Christmas or spring break?"

Bernadette checked her watch. "I have time to drive you home," she said. "Unless you've made an arrangement with Gabe—"

"No, I haven't. I'd appreciate a ride, Bernie." She reached out to take the bill from the returning waiter, but Bernadette snapped it up. "My treat, Angel. You can get it next time."

As soon as Bernadette dropped her off at home, Angel went upstairs to lie down. She hadn't mentioned to Bernie that her head had begun to throb. She took a headache pill and partially closed the wooden blinds but left the window open, feeling relaxed by the sound of the rushing waves breaking on the beach. Stretching out on her bed, Angel tried to focus on deep breathing, but her thoughts kept meandering from the lawyer's meeting to Gabe, and from Gabe to Bernadette.

"Oh Gramsy," she murmured. "I'm so overwhelmed..."

She rolled to one side and hugged her pillow. *You're complicating things,* an inner voice intruded into her thoughts. *Just sign the papers, have the reception for Gramsy and then go back to your life in Toronto, your world. A year will go by fast enough, as you always find when you're teaching. And if you want to return to Chéticamp during the Christmas or spring break, what's stopping you?*

"Gabe," she murmured. *He* was the one stopping her from having peace of mind now, so how could she expect anything different if she returned? How could she switch off the currents that seemed to run through her when she was near him? Currents that only *she* felt, obviously. She couldn't forget the way he had jerked his hand away from hers when they had brushed against each other on the beach.

He was interested in the B&B, not her.

Angel put her fingers up to her temples. She could feel the throbbing of each pulse. "Stop thinking!" she admonished herself. Her thoughts were neither productive nor inspiring.

She squeezed her eyes shut. She hadn't been looking for a man, and what were the chances that she'd feel sparks for Gabe again when she returned to Chéticamp? Someone she had played with as a child, for heaven's sake, and who had given her hope on her sixteenth birthday only to stay away for ten years? Life wasn't fair. Then the universe had thrown Colin her way, which ended up being a total bust, and now Gabe was literally next door to her and figuring in her life in more ways than one.

Ways that she had to ignore, with the hope that he wouldn't haunt her thoughts after she returned to Toronto.

Gabe was speechless for a moment, his gaze taking in the perfectly coiffed, perfectly dressed and perfectly manicured woman he had spent a whirlwind six months with—including two months of engagement—before she broke things off. *What was she doing here, halfway around the world from Scotland? It was a long way to travel just to apologize. If that was her intent.*

He stood up. "Charlotte. It's...uh...been a while." He tried to muster a smile, but couldn't.

"Gabe, I'll understand if you don't want to talk to me." She tossed back her long, red hair. She was a burst of color, with the flared sleeves and pant legs of her green jumpsuit adding the touch of sophistication always displayed in her wardrobe choices.

He pursed his lips. "It's been three years, Charlotte."

She raised a sculpted eyebrow. "I'm very

aware of that, Gabe. So... May I sit for a few minutes?"

Gabe inclined his head and gestured at the empty seat across him. As Charlotte settled in her seat, he felt a strange sensation running through him. He looked up and saw Chris approaching with his seafood chowder and biscuits, and swiftly put up his hand and shook his head. Chris glanced quickly at Charlotte and then gave Gabe a slight nod before returning to the kitchen. Chris would have recognized her from photos Gabe had shared with him. Photos Gabe deleted from his phone when he got home.

Charlotte's green eyes were fixed on him. They were actually brown, but she sometimes changed the color of her contact lenses to match the outfit she was wearing. Gabe had found it somewhat disconcerting at times, gazing into black, blue, hazel or green eyes over the time they were with each other. He rarely saw her brown eyes. Or natural brown hair. When they were dating, she was a strawberry blonde, but changed to a deep auburn red after they were engaged.

She cleared her throat. "Gabe, this is long overdue."

He cocked his head at her and said nothing.

"I... I really should have contacted you much earlier." She waited for him to reply, and when he didn't, she tapped the table nervously with her glossy red fingernails and eyed him squarely. "To apologize. *Sincerely.*"

Gabe wondered how he should reply. *It's kind of too late, don't you think? Why bother, Charlotte? I've gone on with life.* Or: *Why did you bother to come all this way? You could have called or texted...three years ago.*

He frowned. "I've moved on, Charlotte." He looked away from her to the waves chasing each other toward the shore.

"I actually tried to contact you a year ago," she said softly.

Still too late. He turned his gaze back to her.

"I stopped in at Maeve's and I was told you had relocated to Cape Breton Island. I gave up, not having the nerve to call or text."

"You gave up on me two years earlier when I needed your support," Gabe said quietly.

"Look, Gabe. What I did was inexcusable. *Insensitive.* Unforgivable, really." She shook her head, her brow creasing. "I'm sorry I wasn't able to be there for you. I was selfish, I wasn't patient with the grieving process you were going through." She bit her lip and tried to blink back tears. She reached for a handkerchief and dabbed carefully at her eyes.

He opened his mouth to reply but she held up her hand.

"No, please let me finish, Gabe. I have a client who wants to purchase property here, so I thought I'd take the chance to come in person to apologize to you. I want to let you know that I'm sorry I didn't have the empathy I should have had when you were grieving." She threw up her hands. "I had never lost anybody until my dad died six months ago. Now I can only imagine how painful it must have been for you to lose both your parents at the same time. I should have been more understanding, more patient with your grieving process." She took a deep breath. "I'm truly sorry for having caused you even more grief. I couldn't live with myself if I didn't try to make amends."

"I'm really sorry for your loss, Charlotte," Gabe murmured. "Your dad was a great guy."

Charlotte nodded. "Thanks, Gabe. He was a great guy and a wonderful father." She wiped her eyes again. "You know, he was really upset at me when I told him that I had broken things off and that we were no longer together." She shook her head. "He said I had let a good man get away."

Gabe felt a twinge in his chest. He gazed at Charlotte helplessly. The past was past, and there was no changing things now.

"I can see that now, Gabe." Charlotte intertwined her hands as if in prayer. "Can you find it in your heart to forgive me?"

Gabe let out a breath he'd been subconsciously holding in. His thoughts were racing as fast as his pulse. He gazed out the window and the image of Angel at the beach beside him popped up in his mind. Another twinge. In less than two weeks, she'd be gone.

He turned back to meet Charlotte's hopeful gaze. "I've forgiven you, Charlotte. I don't hold any grudges."

She blinked, almost as if she couldn't believe what he was saying. "Thank you. Would you be willing to give us another chance, Gabe?" she said softly, her green eyes glistening.

CHAPTER FIFTEEN

Angel's eyes fluttered open. Disoriented, she stared at the ceiling for a few seconds. And then she remembered lying down after Bernadette drove her home.

She reached for her phone on her night table and checked the time. *How could it be after four?* She'd nodded off for over two hours. Running her fingers through her hair, she strode to the washroom to freshen up.

Feeling more revived in the kitchen after drinking a glass of orange juice, Angel tried to decide whether to go through Gramsy's cooking binders or to just inspect each room and make a list of the items she couldn't part with. Either task would take a chunk of time, and now that the sun was streaming through the windows, Angel was tempted to leave both tasks for the next rainy day. She might as well take advantage of the sun and heat while it lasted, and go for a relaxing swim. She would cook up something for herself after that, if she even felt hungry at all. She was still full from lunch with Bernadette.

Angel had brought the suitcase she had originally packed before getting the news that Gramsy had passed. It had a couple of bathing suits in it, summer wear, a few dressy items and, now, a special dress for the reception for Gramsy. Sifting through it, she pulled out a tangerine one-piece bathing suit and quickly changed into it. She packed an oversize towel in her beach bag, her beach hat and a bottle of sunscreen after applying it to her face and body.

Since Gabe would be working at his restaurant, she'd have a long stretch of beach to herself. It was rare to have people wander toward their end of the island, and Angel was looking forward to having some alone time. She decided to bring along a beach chair and, just as she did whenever she visited in the past, a book and a couple of locking bags for any stones and shells she collected.

With a shiver of excitement, Angel put on her swimsuit cover-up and beach shoes, and headed down to the beach. The sun and heat had intensified during the day and it felt good after the bouts of wind and rain. She lifted her face and gazed at the endless expanse of azure sky. Not a cloud in sight. She breathed in the salt-tinged ocean air and exhaled slowly, feeling the last vestiges of stress from the morning start to dissipate.

Angel set down the folding chair and her other items. The water would be cold—it always was in the summer—so she'd go for a walk first and get toasty warm before diving in for a swim. After grabbing her shell and stone-collecting bags, she began her walk. The gentle and repetitive swoosh of the waves nudging the shore was comforting as she scanned the beach sand for her treasures. She stayed close to the water's edge so she could rinse off any shell or stone before slipping it into one of her bags. She loved the way the colors of the rocks would pop when rinsed. As a child, she would imagine that they were ocean jewels that she had discovered, their shiny hues resembling some of the vibrant colors in her box of crayons. Gramsy had kept her prized collections over the years, displayed in various bowls and dishes around the B&B.

And she had kept the heart-shaped shell Gabe had given her, only to shove the box in a corner of her bedroom closet after communication between them had dwindled and then ceased.

Angel straightened and turned to look at the house that she had been coming to for almost three decades. Her summer visits to Gramsy had been her birthday gift from her parents. Sometimes they accompanied her, but their work schedules did not always allow them to take holidays at the same time. So sometimes she traveled with one parent, and sometimes alone. Angel had no problem traveling alone. Whether they went by train or plane, she always enjoyed the journey.

A series of raucous cries diverted her attention, and she turned to see the descent of a black-and-white seabird on the water. A common murre, with its distinctive black head and body, and white underside. She was wistful as she watched it, wondering what it would be like, not having all this to return to in the summer. Gabe's estate came into her peripheral vision and she turned to gaze at its multiple gables, upper-floor decks and huge scenic windows. The groomed path from the home to the shoreline brought back memories of Gabe helping her as she limped into the house after injuring her leg. And then her mind became flooded with images of moments with Gabe.

Angel shook her head and walked briskly on, focusing on thoughts about the reception to celebrate Gramsy's life. She wanted to go through the photo albums on the bottom shelf of one of the living room bookshelves and compile photos to put into a slide presentation on her laptop. She could have it running on a loop while friends popped in to pay their respects. And in the next couple of days, she'd make some cookies, scones and loaves to serve with coffee and tea.

By the time Angel turned around and returned to her beach chair, she was sweltering. She poked around in her bag for a hair elastic and swept back her hair into a ponytail before taking off her cover-up. She eyed the undulating waves, and knowing it was better to dash into the water instead of inching into it slowly, she gave a whoop and ran for it.

She gasped at the first impact of the water, but she continued immersing herself, head included. She came up to the surface and treaded water while getting used to the exhilaratingly cold-water temperature. She knew that the initial numbness would gradually fade after her body acclimatized. When it did, she swam parallel to the coastline for a bit and then floated, loving the gentle buoyancy of the waves.

The sun on her face and the silky water cradling her body filled her with a sense of peace and relaxation. *What a gift to have the waters of the Gulf of Saint Lawrence practically in Gramsy's backyard.* Angel breathed in the fresh breeze and wished she could float for hours. She was tempted to close her eyes, and she did, briefly, but she knew she had to stay attentive, or she'd be transported too far from the shore. She was a pretty good swimmer, but she wasn't about to get overconfident with the deeper waters.

Angel reverted to swim mode for another stretch and then turned back toward Gramsy's neck of the beach. When her feet touched bottom, she proceeded to walk her way out of the water. Squinting in the sun, she saw a figure approaching on the beach. She wiped her eyes and the figure came clearly into view.

Gabe. Wearing swimming trunks and with a plush towel draped over one shoulder. She stopped, well aware of the water dripping from her shivering body and still too far to grab her beach towel.

Gabe felt an erratic drumming in his chest at the sight of Angel emerging from the water in her iridescent orange swimsuit. He hoped she hadn't noticed his fleeting gaze sweeping over her seconds earlier. The last thing he wanted was for her to feel uncomfortable with him.

"Hi, Angel," he called out casually, also coming to a stop.

"Hi," she said, and strode swiftly to her beach chair to grab her towel and drape it around herself.

He was still a few paces away but he didn't advance. "I guess we both got the same memo—'Sun's out; go for a swim.'"

Angel held the towel tightly against her. "I thought you would be at your restaurant. Not that it would matter if you weren't. I mean—"

"I was at Mara's earlier…with someone I knew. And then I decided I needed a quick break before returning for the evening."

Gabe had been taken aback by Charlotte's appearance and even more so by her wanting to know if there was still a chance for them. He had excused himself for a few moments and had sought out Chris privately to briefly explain the situation. Chris had generously offered to take his evening shift so Gabe could deal with his ex-fiancée, and Gabe was genuinely touched, but he told Chris that he wouldn't return as early as he usually did, but he'd still be in for the evening shift. Returning to the booth, he suggested taking Charlotte to a nearby park to have a more private conversation. She agreed.

Gabe didn't want to think about their discussion now. He just wanted to cool off with an invigorating swim before heading back to Mara's. However, he hadn't expected to see Angel here. "I hope you don't mind if I go for a quick swim? I don't want to intrude on your privacy…"

"This isn't my private beach," she said, sitting on her chair with her towel still around her. "Go for it." Her gaze dropped to his chest before quickly shifting to her bag to grab a book.

Gabe glanced at the title: *Fairies and Fables of Cape Breton Island.* His mouth twitched. "I recognize that book. You would read it on the bluff the summer that we—"

"You remember that?" Angel stared at him incredulously.

"I do," he said, unable to hold back a smile. "After reading about the fairy dances, you were bound and determined to spot them on their fairy hills."

"I was a kid. Kids believe in magic." She shrugged. "I saw the book in my room and was curious." She opened it and looked intently at the illustration next to the title page.

Gabe took the hint. "Enjoy the read. Or reread. Maybe it'll make you believe in magic again." He walked toward the water and tossed his towel far enough on the beach to avoid the surf's reach. When he glanced back at Angel, she was still looking at her book. He turned, but not before catching her looking up from the page.

Feeling a surge of heat spiraling through his body, Gabe made a run for the bracing waters and dived in without hesitation.

CHAPTER SIXTEEN

ANGEL WAS EMBARRASSED that Gabe had caught her watching him. She wished she could quietly leave but she was reluctant to show him that his appearance had affected her. She set the beach chair in the lounging position and put on her cover-up. Lying back, she started reading her book, but thoughts and images of Gabe kept shattering her concentration. The last person she had expected to encounter on the beach was Gabe, looking like "Mr. August" in a firefighter calendar.

How could she stop the fluttering in her chest? And why was her body betraying her? She told herself that it was normal to admire a perfect physique, whether it belonged to a man or a woman.

But her reaction wasn't normal.

Just looking at Gabe gave her a rush that she had never experienced with anyone else, not even Colin. Yes, she had been attracted to Colin, but her nerve endings hadn't sparked when she saw him, like they did with Gabe. And any superficial attraction she had felt for Colin had dissolved instantly when she found out that he was married.

So why did she tingle all over, blood pulsing through her veins, feeling a yearning that coursed from her core upward when she was around Gabe?

Because maybe you want him?

Angel closed her book with a snap, and stared at it in shock. How could she be having these crazy thoughts? The sun must be getting to her. She looked up, her heart jolting wildly as Gabe emerged from his swim. She couldn't pull her gaze away. He bent to reach for his towel, his arm muscles flexing. He shook it out and towel-dried his hair before quickly running it over his body.

She averted her gaze when he wrapped the towel around his hips and started walking toward her. Stopping a few paces away, he said, "Mind if I join you for a minute?"

Angel cleared her throat and gazed up at him. "No problem."

It was more than a problem.

Even a minute was dangerous. The more time she was around Gabe, the more she realized that something was chipping away at her convictions. The conviction that she had to sell the B&B and return to Toronto. The belief that she couldn't possibly have serious feelings for Gabe. Again. Feelings that went beyond just wanting to enjoy his body...

Angel didn't want to even formulate the words in her mind. Because it wasn't ever going to happen. She'd be crazy to believe for even a minute that it would.

Gabe laid his towel on the beach parallel to her lounge chair and stretched out on it, his hands tucked under his head as he looked up at the sky. "Would you like to have dinner at Mara's tonight?" he said casually.

Angel's heart skipped a beat. She leaned over slightly and her book slipped out of her hands onto the sand between her and Gabe. She reached over to get it and gave a yelp as she leaned too far and found herself tumbling over herself, ending up pressed up against Gabe with his arms flying out involuntarily to help her.

The impact took her breath away as she lay against him, his arms bracing her.

She didn't move, and neither did he.

"Are you okay?" Gabe murmured, his mouth brushing against her temple.

What was happening? She shifted slightly and his teal-green gaze was on her, his brow furrowed in concern. His mouth, oh so close. Angel couldn't speak, and for a moment she wondered if she had banged her head and was rendered speechless with a concussion. Was she imagining the intensity in his eyes? The desire? The sensation of their bodies pressed together was... breathtaking. Her mouth opened in wonder and Gabe promptly kissed her. *Slowly.* Tenderly. And when she started to respond to his touch, he cradled her head with one hand and his kiss became more passionate.

When he pulled away, his breath ragged, alarm bells rang in her mind.

"Are you okay?" he huskily repeated his earlier question. "Did you hurt yourself?"

Angel shifted away from him, her mind a jumble of emotions. "I... I'll be okay." She cringed as she stood up. "I'm more embarrassed than hurt." She put her book in the bag and closed up the lawn chair.

"Don't be, Angel," he said gruffly. "It was an accident. And I'm very sorry. I got caught up in the moment." He rose. "I should go and get ready for my shift." He shook out his towel and wrapped it around his waist. "I'd really like you to check out Mara's, Angel. I'll be busy with an engagement dinner tonight, but I guarantee you'll love the food." Angel hesitated for a moment, wondering how wise this would be. She had let herself get carried away with Gabe and now she was regretting it. Their attraction had been mutual, yes, but the reality was that she was still leaving Chéticamp Island. She couldn't afford to get tangled up with Gabe physically or emotionally. She'd have to make it clear to him that her focus for the remainder of her time on the island was to get things ready for Gramsy's reception.

In any case, if she went to Mara's with him, she'd be dining alone, which would be safe. Then she'd take a cab home, instead of waiting for him to finish his shift. "Okay, I did want to check out Mara's before I left," she said casually, heading to the path back to Gramsy's.

"Great. Can I come by and pick you up in about forty minutes?"

His words followed her as she walked away, and she was pretty sure his gaze was following her, too.

Gabe watched Angel for a few moments before heading to the path back to his place. His heart was still hammering against his chest. Angel had literally fallen into his arms, and he had responded automatically, his senses instantly charged by the feel of her face and body touching his.

He should have shown more control...

But his instincts had taken over, overwhelming him with all the feelings that he had kept locked up inside him: protectiveness, desire and the need for human connection. *Connection with a woman. Physically and emotionally.*

When his lips brushed her temple, the feel of her soft skin ignited him instantly. Feeling the length of her body against his had sent him into another realm. He didn't have to say anything to reveal how his body was responding. The way she had gazed at him, eyes and mouth open, had done him in. He wanted to hold her, taste her lips, feel her heart beating against his.

Their kisses hadn't been the sweet ones shared on her sixteenth birthday. These were the passionate kisses of two adults wanting more, needing more.

With the feel of the sun on his body and the sensual sound of the rushing waves, Gabe had lost himself in the moment. Time stood still when he kissed her, and feeling her responding had inflamed him even more. When a niggling voice in his mind warned him that things could get out of control for both of them, he'd reluctantly pulled away. In an unexplainable way, he felt responsible for Angel while she was on the island, and the weight of the reason she was here in the first place had brought an abrupt halt to his passion.

After stepping inside, Gabe threw the beach towel in the laundry room and headed upstairs.

He checked the time and then headed for the shower, his thoughts alternating between Angel and Charlotte. Before they both reappeared in his life, he had mainly focused on one thing: his restaurants. He took his role and reputation as a Michelin-starred chef seriously, and working at his profession took up most of his time, especially since he flew back to Scotland regularly to check on operations at Maeve's.

Charlotte.

Her appearance at Mara's had shocked the hell out of him. And her apology and desire for reconciliation even more. Noticing the restaurant starting to fill in, he wanted to find a more private space to talk. They left Mara's, with several curious gazes directed mostly at Charlotte. The tongues of the regulars would be wagging, no doubt. He had laughed on several occasions when Bernadette told him that he was Inverness County's most eligible bachelor, and that his Scottish brogue and handsome beard had the single ladies sighing and vying for his attention.

Which is why he had mostly avoided attending the year-round local *cèilidhs*, rollicking nights of fiddle music and dancing, whether in a hall, barn or other community space. Not that he didn't enjoy this Celtic tradition; it was just that he hadn't been motivated to engage in that kind of fun as a single person. Perhaps he'd change his mind when he was lucky enough to find the right person to go with, he told Bernadette with a smirk.

And how will you meet anyone if you're always cooking in your restaurant or home, Chef? Bernadette had challenged him good-naturedly. *You have to get your Scottish buns out there, laddie.*

Gabe had opened the side door of his Porsche for Charlotte and drove to the nearest park. It felt awkward to have her in the front seat, especially since Angel had been the only woman—other than Gramsy—who had occupied that spot since he had moved to the island. And the awkward silence between him and Charlotte intensified his unease.

He was thankful for the hot weather, which meant they could sit at one of the shaded park benches instead of staying in the car. When they arrived, there were only a few people strolling or jogging on the grounds.

When they were both seated, Charlotte tossed her hair back and looked at him with a rueful smile. "I'm sorry for just showing up like I did, Gabe. But I couldn't take the chance that you would refuse to see me." She sighed. "And I really wanted—*needed*—to apologize for abandoning you in your time of need." She shook her head. "Your forgiveness means a lot to me."

Gabe rubbed his jaw. "I'm not a saint, Charlotte. I was upset when I got your note and ring. More than upset. Shocked. Hurt. Disappointed. And maybe angry for a while. But I was dealing with enough grief over losing my parents." He looked away, his jaw tensing.

"I'm sorry."

He held up a hand. "It's done with, no need to apologize again." He met her gaze. "Life went on."

"I missed you, Gabe."

Gabe couldn't bring himself to say "I missed you, too." Maybe because he had been too numb at the time to miss her.

"We had something once, Gabe. I think we could have something better now." She put a hand on his arm briefly. "I want to try to make it up to you, if you let me." She blinked, trying to hold back tears. "Unless there's someone in your life…?"

Gabe almost wanted to laugh. How was he supposed to answer that? *Um, kind of, but she's about to leave, so there's no chance of anything developing.* "Not really," he said, "but—"

"You don't have to explain," she said. "Gabe, I want to earn back your trust. All I'm asking is for you to give me a chance. I'm here for a week on business and then I have another week off for myself. Maybe we could get together some evening this week?" Her green eyes were hopeful. "I've changed, Gabe. In the ways I needed to change."

"I've changed, too, Charlotte," he said quietly. "I just don't think we can go back in time."

She shook her head. "We wouldn't be going back, Gabe. We'd be going forward. Like you said, the past is done with."

Gabe inhaled and exhaled deeply. Charlotte looked as attractive as she had in the past, but there *was* something different about her. Her humility, for one. Could he entertain the thought of giving her a chance? Trust her again? He was being honest when he told her that he had forgiven her. But forgiving didn't mean forgetting.

"One day at a time, Gabe."

He started. It was almost as if she had read his thoughts. "I don't want to give you false hopes, Charlotte." He glanced at his watch. "I need to head back home. I have things to do before I get ready for my shift tonight."

She gazed at him for a few seconds, then nodded. "I'll have lunch at Mara's and then I'll take a cab back to my hotel."

"May I offer you a ride?" he said lightly.

She smiled. "You may."

When they arrived at Mara's, Charlotte turned

to Gabe. "*Tapadh leat*," she murmured and squeezed his hand before letting herself out. "I think I'll go in for a bowl of the seafood chowder. I checked the website and saw that it's a favorite with customers."

Gabe couldn't bring himself to reply to their Scottish Gaelic "Thank you." He smiled politely and nodded, and when she entered the restaurant, he left immediately for home, intending to decompress with a refreshing swim before his shift.

Only he hadn't imagined encountering Angel on the beach—

And now, as he showered, Gabe tried to suppress images of Angel from his mind and concentrate instead on the evening's menu at Mara's.

But his mind wouldn't let him.

CHAPTER SEVENTEEN

Why had she said yes to going to Mara's with Gabe?

And how could she face Gabe again after what had happened between them? She shook her head. No, she couldn't see him again. At least not so soon. She turned off the blow dryer and set it down before pacing around her room in her bathrobe. What excuse could she use?

Before she could think of anything, her cell phone rang. Her nerves taut, and wondering if that was Gabe now, she picked it up. Bernadette, on her last break.

"Thank goodness it's *you*!"

"What's the matter, Angel? Did something happen?"

"Um…yes! And I'm embarrassed to tell you about it, Bernie, but if I don't, I'll burst."

"Oh my gosh, what is it?"

Angel gave Bernadette an edited version of what occurred between her and Gabe. "And I said yes to going to Mara's with him tonight.

He's working, though, so I wouldn't exactly be sitting across from him all night trying to keep my mind off his body. I really should text him and cancel. He could be here any minute and I'm not even dressed."

"Angel! Listen to me. You don't want to miss the chance to eat at Mara's. If you're that uncomfortable with Gabe after what happened, why don't I meet you there once I'm done here? That way, you won't be alone and if Gabe does have time to join you, it will be less awkward with me there. And Gabe won't mind."

"I don't know, Bernie…"

"Angel, really, we're in the twenty-first century. What happened was an accident and then you both succumbed to temptation. At least partially." She laughed. "Which is totally understandable, with both of you being pretty cute, if I may say so. And it's not like it's going to go anywhere, with you leaving in a week and a half…"

"You're right," Angel said swiftly. "It isn't."

"Okay, then. I'll see you in a bit."

"But—"

"No *buts*, Angel. Now go and get dressed. Love you!"

Angel stared at her cell phone for a few moments, then strode to her closet and looked at the limited items she had brought for this trip. She decided on a silky midi dress with tulip sleeves and a scattering of pink and apricot vintage roses. She had liked the feminine look of it, with its fitted waist and flared skirt. Feminine but not provocative.

She didn't want to give Gabe any ideas.

At the sound of tires on the driveway, Angel took a last glance in the mirror and hurried downstairs to put on a pair of ivory lace-up sandals. She rose just as Gabe rang the doorbell.

She opened the door and gave Gabe a tentative smile.

"Hi, Angel. You look very nice," he said casually. "I hope you don't mind if we jet it to Mara's?"

With his crisp white shirt and black trousers, Gabe looked very nice, too, but she couldn't bring herself to repay the compliment.

"Not at all," she said, grabbing her handbag. He strode to open the door of the gleaming silver Porsche for her and waited until she was seated. "Oh, your hem is hanging out," he said, and bent to tuck it inside the car. His hand brushed hers as she did the same. Their gazes met for a few seconds and a sizzle went through her as she tried not to let her gaze slip to his lips. He straightened and shut the door.

On the drive to Mara's, he put on some fiddle music. "That always gets me in the cooking mood," he said with a half grin.

"Somehow, I don't think you need any help to get you in the mood. For cooking," she added hastily. She turned to look out her window, sure that her cheeks were as pink as the roses on her dress.

"You're right," he said, turning down the music. "I love cooking, no matter the time of day or night. And I love cooking with the changing seasons we're lucky to have as Canadians."

"What's your favorite?" Angel said, glancing back at him.

He chuckled. "That's a hard one. I have my specialties for each season. Let me see. Summer is the most abundant one, with fresh fruits and vegetables from our restaurant gardens. And I love fall, where I imitate the colors of the Highlands and the Cabot Trail with my autumn dishes. Winter is a cozy season, perfect for comfort food—" he smiled at Angel "—like lobster mac and cheese."

"You mean you made me a winter dish?" Angel said, feigning disapproval.

"That's an all-season favorite," he laughed. "And you loved it, admit it."

Angel smirked. "And spring?"

"Spring literally puts a spring in everyone's steps. Everyone's out walking, so I keep things light and I experiment with combinations. Cape

Breton meets Tuscany, for example. *Aragosta fiorentina.*"

"Pardon me?"

"Lobster florentine, with arugula instead of spinach, and a creamy lemon and fennel sauce over fettuccine."

"That's light?"

"Touché! Okay, maybe not as light as some of my other dishes. I try to please all tastes," he said, the corners of his eyes crinkling as he smiled.

"You still haven't said which season is your favorite," she said as he turned into the restaurant parking lot and drove into the space marked *RESERVED FOR CHEF GABRIEL.*

"You're going to try to pin me down, eh?" Gabe said teasingly, turning to her. His brows furrowed, as he probably realized the double entendre of his words.

She wanted to melt in her seat.

"Winter's my favorite," he said huskily. "I love to cook when it's snowing outside and while listening to Christmas music, both at Mara's and at home. Having a cozy dinner by my fireplace wearing my reindeer pajamas. And eggnog and Cape Breton pork pies for dessert. *Or butterscotch pie.*"

Angel pictured herself sitting by the roaring

fire with Gabe, wearing her candy-cane pajamas. A cozy season they'd never share.

She gave him a half-hearted smile and turned to open the car door. Why did her heart suddenly feel heavy?

Angel stopped to gaze at the stylized sign bearing Gramsy's first name. Gabe waited beside her. "Do you like it?" he said.

"I do," she replied without shifting her attention from the sign. "I like the way the *M* drops down and becomes a set of waves, with more waves above, directly underneath the rest of her name. Very appropriate. She loved the water and always said she was living her dream when Grampsy built their house on Chéticamp Island." Her voice cracked and she paused and quickly wiped her eyes. "I'm sorry."

Gabe took a step forward so he could face Angel directly. "You don't have to be," he said softly. "Gramsy meant the world to you. And to me. Of course you're going to feel her loss, especially when you're at her place, or when you're reminded of her in some way." He smiled. "She liked the sign, too, but she liked the food in here even more."

Angel laughed. "Of course she did. Now you know where I get my love of food." She gestured toward the front door. "So let me in, Chef, before I huff and I puff and—you know the drill."

"You're funny," he said. "Have you ever considered doing stand-up?"

"I already do. In my classroom," she said, her lips twitching.

Gabe burst out laughing. "Your kids must love you." He pressed the code into the panel by the front door of the restaurant and a buzzer sounded. He opened the door for Angel, and moments later they were in the dining room.

"By the way, Gabe, I was talking to Bernadette and she said she would join me, since you'd be cooking away. She said you wouldn't mind."

"Oh, she did, did she?" He feigned a frown. He supposed he shouldn't feel disappointed. It was unfair of him to expect Angel to dine alone, although he had intended to join her intermittently throughout the evening, especially when she took her first bites of every course. Well, it was probably safer this way. He seemed to keep putting his foot in his mouth whenever he was with her. "Of course I wouldn't mind. Bernadette is the sister I never had." He chuckled as he led Angel to the booth he had occupied earlier. "She's bossy at times, and brutally honest, but I love her. She has a heart of gold. I'm sure you know she has a gig singing and playing guitar two or three times a month at ceilidhs all over Cape Breton Island. The venues are always packed when people know she's performing. Everyone loves her."

"She's easy to love," Angel said. "And funny, I always thought of her as the sister *I* never had."

"Well, speak of the little devil now," he said, glancing out the window. "I just saw her car pull in. It's still too early to open, but I'll let her in and you two can chat while I slave away in the kitchen."

"*You're* funny now," Angel said.

He shrugged and a couple of minutes later he was back with Bernadette. "And now, ladies, I'll have Jeremy come out and offer you some drinks." He turned to Angel. "I'll return in a bit to introduce you to my sous-chef."

Gabe walked briskly to the kitchen. Shortly, he'd switch to chef mode, but while he was donning his white Lafont jacket in a side room, he could allow himself the indulgence of thinking about how lovely Angel looked. *A natural beauty.* And maybe one with a little bit of fairy magic to bewitch unsuspecting chefs with.

If someone had told him a week ago that he'd be falling again for Angel, *and* that his ex-fiancée would be arriving from Scotland and trying to reconcile with him, he would have seriously questioned their sanity.

What was it that people said when confronted with several challenges at once? *It never rains but pours.*

He had some decisions to make, the first being whether or not he should let Angel know about his feelings for her. Not the physical ones. She was already aware of those. But would it even make a difference? Convince her to maybe stay for the rest of the summer and at least see if there was a chance to make it work? That is, if she even *had* any deeper feelings for him.

He sighed. The complicating factor was her teaching. And right now, she couldn't see herself relocating.

And then there was Charlotte, hoping to reignite their relationship. Could he find a way to trust her again? Could he entertain the thought of giving her the benefit of the doubt if there was no way forward with Angel? But how fair would it be to Charlotte, though, to have her waiting on the sidelines while he explored possibilities with Angel?

He wasn't a cad and he had no intentions of playing with their lives. The only thing he could do was to be honest with each of them about his feelings. The question was, whom would he talk to first?

Gabe checked his watch. No more time to think about either Angel or Charlotte. He had some serious cooking to do.

CHAPTER EIGHTEEN

ANGEL LIFTED HER wineglass. "To Gramsy," she said, before clicking her glass with Bernadette's.

"To Gramsy," Bernadette said solemnly.

"Very nice," Angel said after tasting the wine.

"Somebody must be trying to impress you," Bernadette said with a teasing smile.

Angel frowned. "Why do you say that?"

"That happens to be an extremely expensive wine. I know, because it was served at Mara's soft opening for a small group of Gabe's friends, including me and Gramsy."

"Well, I'll only have one glass, then."

"I'm sure Gabe's not going to make you pay, silly. He *did* invite you here, right?"

"Yes, but—"

"Angel, I know he wanted you to enjoy a dinner at the place he named after Gramsy. Enjoy the experience." She leaned across the table conspiratorially. "Is he a good kisser?" she said, lowering her voice.

"Bernie!" Angel looked around self-consciously. "It happened so quickly—"

"And? Come on, you barely gave me any details on the phone. And you've never held back in the past about Colin or any of your other boyfriends."

"Gabe is not my boyfriend. And you make it sound like I had an endless supply of guys in my life. Which I did not!"

"Okay, okay, but from your flushed cheeks, I'm going to infer that he was a great kisser."

"Bernie, you're incorrigible!" Angel said, and laughed at Bernadette's feigned pout. "Okay, I admit it, but it was my fault for falling down and practically landing on top of him."

"Well, you obviously made an impression on each other. *Literally.*" Bernadette grinned.

"It doesn't mean anything, Bernie. And it won't happen again. I'm leaving in a week and a half, remember?"

Bernadette sighed. "I wish you could stay longer. Why don't you extend your trip? Then maybe, you and Gabe—"

"Did I hear my name? Bernie, are you telling tales about me? You know the penalty for that is doing the dishes." Gabe laughed as he approached their booth, followed by his sous-chef, whom he introduced to Angel.

"Nice to meet you, Chris." She smiled and shook his hand.

"The pleasure is mine." He placed his other hand over hers. "I'm sorry for your loss, Angel, and I hope you take comfort in knowing how much Gramsy meant to us here and in the community."

She nodded. "Thank you. I do."

He left and Angel met Gabe's gaze. She wondered if he had heard any of her earlier comments or noticed her gaze inadvertently traveling down the length of him as he approached, drop-dead gorgeous in his white chef's jacket and tailored black trousers.

From the corner of her eye, she could see Bernadette watching them. She gave her a gentle kick under the table.

"Ow!" Bernadette blurted.

Gabe turned to her. "Are you okay?"

"Uh...yeah. Just a cramped muscle in my leg. I'll just walk it off. Be right back."

Angel hoped her burning face didn't give her away.

"Have you had a chance to look at the menu?" Gabe's gaze reverted to her.

She hadn't even glanced at the menu.

"Or would you like it if I surprised you with the selections for your dinner tonight? Perhaps choosing some of Gramsy's favorites?"

"Oh! Sure, why not? Actually, I think that would be very nice." She looked away from him as the memory of what his chest looked like under his jacket made her catch her breath.

"Okay, I'll get right on that."

But he didn't move, and she looked up at him questioningly.

"I'm glad you came, Angel," he said huskily. "I—" He caught sight of Bernadette returning. "I hope you enjoy what I make you."

He met Bernadette on his way back to the kitchen and they exchanged a few words.

"Did he tell you that he's surprising us with his dishes?"

"Yes, I told him I was good with that." Her eyes narrowed. "Did you and Gabe talk about anything else? I figured that's why you kicked me under the table."

"Really? You thought I was giving you a hint to leave?" Angel shook her head. "No, I just noticed you staring at the both of us with that dazed look of wonder, and I wanted you to stop. You didn't have to yell."

"You got me on the shinbone, girlfriend. I almost jumped out of my seat."

"Aw, I'm sorry, Bernie."

"No, you're not," Bernadette laughed. "Now come clean. Did you feel something special when you two collided?"

Angel sighed. "I won't get any peace until I answer, so okay, yes, I felt *something*. And I'm sure he did, too. Something purely physical, nothing else."

Bernadette raised her eyebrows. "Are you sure it was just physical? I was observing the way you and Gabe looked at each other. Call me a romantic fool, but I thought there was something more than just a physical vibe between you two."

Angel was relieved to spot Jeremy walking with a tray toward them. She was reluctant to further analyze her or Gabe's feelings, physical or otherwise, with Bernadette. At least not at the moment.

Jeremy set two parfait glasses in front of them. "Enjoy your appetizer, Chef Gabriel's Inverness shrimp parfait. Chef will check on you shortly."

Angel met Bernadette's gaze after their first taste. "Amazing." The melt-in-your-mouth lime mousse with slivers of lemon zest complemented the grilled shrimp beautifully. "Great taste, Gramsy," she murmured.

They had enjoyed a few mouthfuls when Gabe returned. "I hope the parfaits are to your liking, ladies?" His gaze went from Bernadette to Angel.

"Delicious," Angel said. "I could have this every day."

Bernadette nodded. "Ditto."

Gabe smiled approvingly. "Great. I passed test number one." His gaze remained fixed on Angel. "A few more to go."

Angel dropped her gaze and hoped her cheeks wouldn't betray her reaction to what she perceived as Gabe implying something else...

When Gabe left, Bernadette nudged Angel. "I knew it."

"Knew what?" Angel raised an eyebrow as she bit into a shrimp.

"There is something going on between you two. Gabe couldn't take his eyes off you."

"Oh, come on, Bernie. He was looking at you, too."

"Yeah, for a nanosecond. His eyes were practically smoldering when he was talking to you."

Angel couldn't help laughing. "Bernie, have you considered writing a romance? You have the imagination for it!"

Bernadette was about to answer when her cell phone dinged. She reached into her handbag and read the text. After replying, she set it down on the table and sighed. "Ross is tied up tonight," she said. "We were going to get together after dinner and play some board games. In fact, we were going to ask you to join us."

"So what happened?"

"Well, I knew he was meeting with an out-of-country Realtor this afternoon. She's on Cape

Breton Island to scope out properties for a high-powered client. Apparently she has a personal connection here. Anyway, she wanted Ross to take her to see some of the higher-end properties for sale this evening. He texted to see if that was okay with me."

"Aw, how considerate." Angel smiled. "You're a lucky gal, Bernie."

"And Ross is even luckier." Bernadette grinned. "So how about I drive you to my place and we can see who has board game supremacy?"

Angel hesitated. "Maybe another time, Bernie. I think I'll just have an early night tonight. But thanks. Oh, here comes our next dish."

Jeremy approached and set down two bowls of steaming seafood chowder.

"Chef Gabriel sends his regrets. A large group with a reservation for the private room has just arrived and he'll be extremely busy for the next while. He said he'll try to get back before the end of your dinner."

Angel nodded and smiled. She wasn't about to show her disappointment that Gabe wouldn't be stopping by their table. She could feel Bernadette's gaze on her, but she focused on tasting her chowder.

Chock-full of lobster meat, scallops and a variety of other fish and seafood, it was the best chowder Angel had ever tasted. He'll make his future wife very happy one day.

The unbidden thought shocked her. Why was she even thinking such things?

Gabe focused on making a series of his signature dishes for the large group celebrating a wedding engagement. He had just finished making a special surf 'n' turf platter for Angel and Bernadette, but couldn't spare the time to check in on them at their booth.

While Gabe and his team worked in sync, images of Angel inevitably popped up in his mind, but he had to swiftly nudge them aside. He didn't want to compromise the quality of his dishes due to lack of concentration. He would process his thoughts and feelings later, once he was back home.

Gabe strode to the private room to congratulate the engaged couple. The group clapped when they saw him, and the couple and several family members thanked him enthusiastically for his fabulous dishes and the complimentary bottles of champagne.

He continued into the main dining area, looking forward to seeing if Angel and Bernadette had enjoyed their dinner. They were chatting over coffee and dessert, his "Maritime Berry Pavlova."

"We haven't stopped raving about our dinner tonight, Gabe," Bernadette said, "You set the bar pretty high. I may have to get Ross to take some cooking lessons to keep me happy."

Gabe laughed. "Tell him not to bother with lessons. Just have him take you *here* for dinner." He winked as he caught Angel's gaze.

"I'm good with that," Bernadette declared with a thumbs-up.

They all laughed. Bernadette turned to Angel. "If you're ready, I'll get the bill and then we can head out."

"The bill is covered, Bernie. My treat tonight." Gabe put up a hand as Angel and Bernadette started to protest. "I own the place. I can do what I want." He smiled directly at Angel. "And Gramsy would approve."

"Gabriel McKellar, you're the best," Bernadette said, sliding out of the booth to give him a hug. She turned to Angel, who had risen also. "Are you still wanting to head home?"

"I am," Angel said. "But I'll take you up on the board game challenge another night." She glanced at Gabe. "Thank you for a wonderful dinner. It's very kind of you to cover it."

"It's my good deed of the day," he replied. "And you're very welcome." He turned to Bernadette. "I'm done for the night and Chris will close up, so I'll drive Angel home."

"Oh! Okay," Bernadette said swiftly, oblivious to Angel's surprised expression. "I guess that makes sense, since you're next door to each other." She gave Angel a hug. "Talk tomorrow, okay?"

After she left, Gabe looked at Angel. "Don't go away," he smiled. "I'll be right back."

Once he had deposited his chef's jacket in the side room to be sent to the dry cleaners, Gabe went into the kitchen to pack up a generous wedge of the pavlova for Angel and to thank Chris and his team for another excellent night.

He returned to find Angel in the same spot, tapping her fingers on the table. He handed her the see-through container. When she saw what it was, her eyes lit up.

A flicker of pleasure ran through him. Perhaps the adage about the way to a man's heart could be reversed. And then an inner voice told him not to be foolish. *It would take much more than food to get to Angel's heart.*

"I'm glad you enjoyed my humble offerings tonight," Gabe said as he started up the Porsche.

"I can see why Gramsy spoke so highly of the restaurant. And *you*."

Gabe shot her a surprised glance. "I didn't know I was the subject of your conversations."

"Only very rarely," Angel said in a serious tone.

Gabe caught her teasing grin as she looked

out the window. "Ah. She also mentioned *you* once or twice in the last three years," he returned with a smirk. "Hey, instead of driving you home right away, Angel, I'd like to show you a special spot in the Highlands that I doubt you've been to. And if you have, I'm sure you'll still enjoy it. Sound good?"

"Uh, I'm kind of tired, Gabe. I was intending to just go home and hibernate after eating so much. *Your* fault."

He laughed. She was always making him laugh. "You'll wake up pretty quickly once you see where I'm taking you. Trust me."

She hesitated, her brow creasing.

Those last two words had just popped out of his mouth. Maybe she had trust issues like he did. Gramsy had hinted that Angel had been deceived by a guy she had dated for months. *She broke it off pronto,* she told him approvingly. *My Angel deserves someone better.* Gramsy hadn't revealed the nature of the guy's deception, and Gabe hadn't probed. But now he had to consider whether Angel's hesitation was connected to her past experience with the guy. And with him.

"I suppose I can vary tonight's itinerary slightly," she said. "If it's a short detour. Otherwise, I *will* fall asleep and you'll have no choice but to carry me over Gramsy's threshold. And trust *me*, I weigh much more *now* than when I walked into Mara's." She cocked her head and smiled ruefully.

The image of carrying Angel in his arms sent a current of desire through him. He kept his eyes on the road, not wanting her to see his feelings reflected in his gaze. Things might be different if she was considering a move to the island, but with her future clearly back in Toronto, any attraction he might feel for her, both physical and emotional, could not be encouraged.

CHAPTER NINETEEN

Despite the lively music, Angel felt her eyelids drooping. Had it only been this morning that she and Gabe had seen the lawyer? The emotion of hearing Gramsy's will, meeting Gabe again on the beach and practically smothering him, and then dining at Mara's had pretty well taken up all her mental and emotional reserves. She allowed her eyes to close and the music to drown out her thoughts. She would process things tomorrow, after what she hoped would be a restful sleep.

Though she probably shouldn't have agreed to extending the day with a ride to goodness knows where. Was it wise to be in such close quarters with a guy whose kiss earlier had woken up some part of her that had been numb?

She stifled those thoughts and, keeping her eyes closed, concentrated on the music and the motion of the Porsche as Gabe picked up speed. Minutes later, she felt the car veer to the right and her eyes fluttered open. She squinted to try to see where they were going, but all she could make out was a ribbon of road against a sheer cliff topped by dense woodlands. As the road wound itself around the Highlands, Angel shivered. It was one thing to take the Cabot Trail by day, but by night, the immensity of it was even more daunting, with its cliffs skirting the ocean. She squeezed her eyes shut, feeling lightheaded. "Are we there yet?" she said, her voice cracking.

"We are arriving at the lookout…in five, four, three, two, one." He stopped the car. "You can open your eyes, Angel. And step out of the car. You'll want to see this."

Gabe was staring at her, the corners of his mouth lifting. He jumped out of the Porsche and held her door open. As far as she could see, they were in total darkness, except for the Porsche's interior light. She stepped out of the car and when the door closed and the light went off, she reached for Gabe's arm in alarm, her eyes trying to adjust.

"Now look up, Angel," he said.

She gazed upward and her mouth fell open. She had never seen so many stars in the night sky. Millions and millions. Some tiny, some large, some seeming to twinkle. The Milky Way, the constellations. She stared in awe. Was that Venus? Or Sirius, the brightest star? She did a 360-degree turn. The sheer beauty of it made her eyelids prickle. She blinked and gazed at Gabe.

"I've *never* seen a sky like this. *Ever.* Are we still on earth?"

Gabe laughed softly. "I can't imagine being any closer to heaven than this."

"Wow, I can't get over it. I could stare at the sky all night." She tilted her head up again and as she started to turn, she faltered and Gabe's arms shot out to prevent her from falling. His hands on her bare arms made her catch her breath and when their gazes met, all she could see were stars reflected in his eyes.

"I wanted you to see this before you returned to Toronto," he said huskily. "To remember the beauty of this place, even at night."

Angel swallowed. "I'll never forget this." *And you.* An ache was spreading in her chest as it hit her what and whom she would be leaving behind when she left. The place that had been home to her for a part of practically every summer since she was a kid. Home and a place of magic, with fairy hills and fiddles, and lifetime friends like Bernadette. And maybe the promise of something more with Gabe.

Was it some stellar force that was drawing her closer to him? Making her want to kiss him again? Ignoring all the warning bells in her head, she closed the short distance between them and had barely murmured her thanks when his hands shifted to draw her into his embrace.

Their cheeks brushed against each other briefly and she heard Gabe draw in his breath before their lips met.

Angel threw caution to the wind and returned his kiss readily, pressing her hands against his broad back. His hand reached up to cradle her head and she shivered with pleasure as his lips trailed kisses down her neck slowly and made their way back to her mouth. They finally drew apart as a cool gust of wind swept over them.

"I better get you home," Gabe murmured, his eyes searing into hers.

"Why?" Angel said breathlessly.

"Because you're dangerous. And the stars aren't helping."

"It's your fault for bringing me here."

Gabe stared at her for a moment and then, without warning, swept her up in his arms and swung her around. She gave a yelp that seemed to echo into the Highlands and clasped her hands around his neck.

"Aye, you're right," he drawled, his Scottish brogue sounding even sexier. "And I rightly take all the blame." He set her down gently. "But I can't let you bewitch me any further, or we'll be both sleeping under the stars tonight."

Angel's heart gave a jolt. He was right. If they didn't leave now, any sanity that she still had would leave her. And the stars wouldn't help.

* * *

Gramsy's words came back to Gabe as he drove. *My Angel deserves someone better.* Gramsy had trusted him to help Angel through the process of settling her estate, and he didn't want to do anything to jeopardize that trust. Yet he had allowed himself to be swept away by Angel, once on the beach, and now, under the stars. And from what he had seen and felt, Angel had willingly capitulated to the chemistry between them as well.

They were both vulnerable, having lost Gramsy. And maybe the natural human instinct was to connect with someone who had or who was experiencing similar emotions. But did the feelings that had emerged between him and Angel fall under that category?

It doesn't matter. You can't allow them to go any further.

Gabe felt a twinge in his chest, knowing he had to repress his feelings for Angel in the time that she had left on the island. Keep her at arm's length.

Not an easy task, considering that they had to work things out about the sale of the B&B.

He glanced over at Angel, but she was looking out her window. Not that she could see much in the dark. He wondered if perhaps she, too, had come to the conclusion that it was best to not encourage their budding feelings.

Like it or not, he'd have to come to terms with this reality, as well as the situation that was brewing with Charlotte. Somehow, he had the impression that she wasn't going to give up so easily. She had flown across the world to clear things up with him, for heaven's sake. Could he just casually dismiss her, let her know that it was too late to try to fix things? That it was finished three years ago? He had told her he'd moved on. But he didn't want to think any more about Charlotte now, with Angel sitting next to him. Doing so almost felt like a betrayal to Angel.

The silence between them was getting to him. Had he offended her in some way? Disappointed her?

"Do you want to talk, Angel?" He glanced over at her briefly. "About the meeting with the lawyer. Or *anything else*?"

She inhaled and exhaled deeply. "I don't know. I'm so…mixed up about things."

"About selling the B&B?"

"Hmm. Partially. A part of me wants to cling to it physically, and to all the memories it holds. Another part of me feels guilty that I haven't been back for three years, missing out on Gramsy's last years." Her brow furrowed and she looked away.

When she glanced back at him, she was blinking away tears.

"Angel, Gramsy was proud of you for being such a dedicated teacher, taking those summer courses to benefit your students. She wouldn't want you to feel guilty."

"She probably should have left something to you, having helped her so much."

Gabe took the exit into Chéticamp. "Angel, I owe a debt of gratitude to Gramsy. She inspired me to become the chef that I am. That was her gift to me, along with treating me like a grandson, and I'll never forget it. That's why I wanted to honor her by having a restaurant built in her name." He chuckled softly. "I'm not lacking for anything, Angel, and when Gramsy asked me if there was anything I wanted, I told her that she had already given me everything a grandson could want. Her love and attention. *Her recipes*," he added with a smile. "So don't feel bad or guilty about anything. The B&B is rightfully yours."

Angel didn't reply and looked ahead while they passed the familiar spots on Main Street, Le Gabriel Restaurant and Evangeline's, places she had often been to during her summer visits, their names evoking Longfellow's epic poem that she had read several times.

"But Gramsy also knew that if you intended to sell," he continued, "I would want the B&B. She knew how much it meant to me, too." Gabe turned at the beach sign and, a few minutes later, came to a stop in Gramsy's driveway. "If and when you're ready, Angel," he said, meeting her gaze, "just name your price and I'll empty my piggy bank."

His heart lifted when she laughed softly.

"You make me laugh, even when I don't want to."

"I don't mind being laughed at." Gabe grinned. *Or kissed*, he wished he could tell her. He also wished he could reach over and give her a reassuring hug.

A sudden ring startled them both, and their gazes shifted to Gabe's cell phone in the open console between them. The caller's name was visible to both of them. *Charlotte*.

"I'll say good-night," Angel said quickly, letting herself out of the Porsche.

"Hold on, Angel," Gabe called out, but she was already at her doorstep. Frowning as the cell phone kept ringing, he watched Angel disappear into the house. "*Damn*," he muttered, and picked up his phone.

CHAPTER TWENTY

ANGEL LOCKED THE door and moments later heard Gabe leaving.

Charlotte. So there was a woman in his life.

But why did that name ring a bell? Where had she seen or heard it before?

Gramsy. Yes, Gramsy had mentioned the name when she was telling Angel about Gabe's tragic loss of his parents and his breakup. That was three years ago.

She remembered feeling for Gabe, even though she hadn't seen him for ten years. Angel felt a knot in her stomach. They were still in touch with each other.

She stared at the container she was holding with the piece of pavlova. She had contemplated having it as a bedtime snack, but her appetite had faded, her stomach too jittery. She strode to the kitchen to put the container in the fridge. Too tired to even think of running a bath, she brushed her teeth, changed into a teddy and got into bed.

Angel flipped her pillow over and turned on her right side to stare out her window at the stars. She breathed the night air deeply, trying to calm her racing thoughts.

Up until seeing Charlotte's name, Angel had been replaying in her mind the scene of Gabe and her gazing at the sky, brimming with a zillion stars that she was sure were sprinkling their magic over them. Gabe's magical kiss had led her to have crazy thoughts and feelings. Thoughts about what it might be like if she stayed longer in Chéticamp. Just a few weeks, to see if the returning spark she felt for Gabe—and that he seemed to reciprocate—would ignite into something more serious. It was crazy. Crazy to have even allowed her mind to veer into these danger zones. Crazy because Gabe obviously still had a connection with his ex-fiancée.

So why did he kiss me? And in a way that was far from casual...

Her heart twisted. Maybe Gabe and Charlotte were a thing again. And *she* had just been a diversion.

Just like she'd been to Colin.

Her eyes started to prickle. She felt hurt, used. Embarrassed by the way she had responded to Gabe's kisses. She turned over on her left side so she wouldn't see the stars. Earlier, they had tricked her into thinking that there was *something* between her and Gabe.

And Gabe had played along.

Angel let the tears flow. It was her fault for letting her guard down, and Gabe was equally to blame. She just didn't know how she was going to face him in the time she had left before flying back to Toronto. There was still the terms of the B&B to finalize, but maybe she could go and see the lawyer herself and sign the necessary papers without Gabe being there. She didn't even want to think about the reception to honor Gramsy at the B&B. Tomorrow, when her head was clear, she would figure out how to deal with that.

Angel flipped the pillow over to the dry side and closed her eyes, concentrating on imagining every room in the B&B, and thinking of the items she wanted to bring back with her or have shipped to Toronto. Tomorrow she would go and purchase some packing boxes.

And the first thing she'd pack up were Gramsy's recipe binders.

Angel's eyes flew open when she realized that the train sound she was hearing was the sound of Bernadette texting. She reached for her phone and squinted to read the message.

Are you up? I have coffee and croissants, right outside your door.

Coming!

Angel slipped out of bed, put on her robe and hurried downstairs. When she opened the door, Bernadette gazed at her with raised eyebrows.

"Late night, Angel?" Her mouth twitched.

"It's not what you think," Angel said, grabbing the bag of croissants. *Not. At. All.* " She opened the door for Bernadette. "Come on in. Coffee first, talk after."

A few minutes later, sitting across from each other at the island, Angel frowned at Bernadette. "Aren't you supposed to be at work?"

"It's Saturday, remember? I'm working the afternoon shift. And hopefully afterward, I'll finally get to see Ross."

"What do you mean, *finally*? Where has he been?"

"He's been spending a lot of time with that out-of-country Realtor I mentioned the other day, showing her properties for her uber-rich client from Edinburgh."

Something clicked in Angel's memory. She put down her half-bitten croissant, her throat suddenly feeling dry. "The one who has a personal connection here?"

"Good memory. Yeah, why?"

Angel felt a twinge in her chest. "Did Ross mention her name?"

"No. Angel, you look really pale. Did you not sleep last night?"

"Not much, no. Can you do me a favor, Bernie? Text Ross and just ask him the name of the Realtor. I think she's—"

"Oh my gosh. Are you thinking what never crossed my mind until now?" Bernadette set down her mug. "That she's—"

"Gabe's ex-fiancée," Angel blurted. "And I think they're back together."

Bernadette shook her head. "I can't believe that. Any time I've met Gabe for coffee or lunch, he never mentioned Charlotte or even hinted at a reconciliation between them. This must be a coincidence. Ross has had other Realtors from the UK scoping out properties here."

"Bernie, when Gabe drove me home last night, he got a call. I saw the caller's name. *Charlotte*."

Bernadette's mouth dropped. She shook her head. "Okay, I'm texting Ross."

A couple of minutes later, she looked up from her phone, her eyes wide. "You're right, Angel. Charlotte's the Realtor he's been dealing with. He's on his way to pick her up at her hotel." She scrunched up her face. "She *is* looking around at properties for a client, but Ross said she was actually considering purchasing a property for herself on the island."

Angel felt as if someone had punched her in the stomach. "I don't think she's joking, Bernie," she said, unable to stop her voice from breaking.

Bernadette stared at her for a moment, eyes widening. "Oh, Angel, you've fallen for him again," she said slowly.

Angel's eyes blurred. "Yeah," she said bitterly. "You can call me 'a fallen angel.'" She wiped her eyes with the napkin from the croissant bag. "And a damn fool."

Gabe stared out the living room window at the beach, willing Angel to appear. She had left the car so abruptly last night. But what did he expect? She had seen the call come through, and if he were to guess, Charlotte's name might have thrown her off. Made her think that he and his ex were on closer terms than they actually were.

That is, if she even knew that Charlotte was his ex-fiancée.

He couldn't blame Angel if she thought he was a cad, kissing her when he was seeing someone else. He had wanted to clear up any misunderstanding right then and there, but she hadn't given him the chance.

Gabe gulped down the rest of his coffee, tired of his conflicting thoughts. They had interrupted his sleep several times last night and he needed to get his act together, especially since there was an invitation-only event at his restaurant tonight. He needed to be in top form, especially since his sous-chef had heard that an international food critic would be among the invited guests.

Pouring his second cup, Gabe went over the last conversation he had with Angel. It had touched him that Angel felt Gramsy could have left him something. What Angel didn't know was that Gramsy *had* left him something. Or rather, *someone*. *Her*.

Of course, Gramsy hadn't known that he would have feelings for Angel. Or had she? Was that something that she had hoped would happen, that the two people she loved would connect—or reconnect—when she was gone?

The more Gabe thought about it, the more it seemed possible that Gramsy had drawn up her will in the way she had for that very reason. He knew she wanted Angel to think about staying in Chéticamp, and Gramsy was wise enough to consider that if Angel felt she had to sell, then she should sell to Gabe. And even wiser—or more cunning—to add the clause about Angel renting the place to him for a year, to give Angel a decent amount of time to really think about whether she wanted to let the B&B and property go.

A memory of Gramsy randomly showing him photos of Angel in the last two years made Gabe suspect now that her actions held a deeper motive. Gramsy knew how much he had suffered after his parents passed and after Charlotte broke up with him. She helped him through his grieving, and was always concerned about him. He would find someone worthy of him and vice versa, she had reassured him. And after treating him to fresh-out-of-the-oven oatcakes or scones, or a steaming seafood chowder, she would casually share her latest photos of Angel. It hadn't hit him then—perhaps his mind and heart were too numb with grief—but now, it seemed more than plausible that Gramsy was trying to be a matchmaker.

This thought made his eyes prickle. Not only had she shown him care and concern—and love—while she was alive, but even after passing, the terms in her will could pave the way for possibilities between him and Angel…

He was going to miss Gramsy dearly. She had been such a good person, not only to him but to her guests and neighbors. He wanted to honor her by doing all the cooking for the reception at the B&B, and he'd hoped to talk about his plans with Angel last night, but she left prematurely.

Perhaps he should make his way over to talk to Angel. Casually tell her that the call coming in last night hadn't meant anything to him. He had to be up front with Angel, explain that his ex-fiancée was in the area for business purposes, and that she was calling to arrange a coffee meeting with him, but that he had politely declined.

But would this even make a difference? Or was he setting himself up for another letdown?

Gabe set down his mug and was about to go upstairs to change out of his robe when the doorbell rang. His pulse spiked, thinking it might be Angel. Perhaps she felt bad for leaving so abruptly last night and was coming over to explain? He strode to the door, not wanting to risk her leaving if he first went up to get dressed.

He tightened the sash on his robe and opened the door. His welcoming smile froze on his face. It was Charlotte.

CHAPTER TWENTY-ONE

ANGEL STRODE TO the living room and plopped down onto one of the recliners. Bernadette sat opposite her.

"Angel, you might have it all wrong, you know," Bernadette said half-heartedly.

Angel shot her a skeptical look. "Come on, Bernie, I'm not that naive."

"Why don't you talk to Gabe and tell him how you feel?"

"You've got to be kidding!" Angel frowned. "I'm not going to embarrass myself any more than I already have." She held up her hand. "I allowed myself to be fooled once. *Not* gonna happen again."

"You can't very well avoid him for the next few days."

"I'll try my best," Angel said decisively. "I want to go out and buy some packing boxes. Can you drive me and give me a hand packing up Gramsy's recipe binders?"

Bernadette sighed. "Well, don't pack up too

much. Gramsy was a wise owl, figuring you needed time to really make up your mind about selling." A gleam came into her eyes. "So maybe there's hope that you will—"

"Bernie, I love you, but don't get your hopes up." She hugged Bernadette. "I'll still visit when I can, and you can come and visit me in Toronto."

"Angel, I love you, too, but don't get *your* hopes up," she said cheekily. "You know I'm not a city girl. I'm a proud Cape Bretoner, and I wouldn't last long without my ocean air and water."

"Yeah, you'd feel like a fish out of water in Toronto," Angel laughed. "Look, Angel. Why don't I just take a run for the boxes, and you can get dressed and call Gabe or just go over?" She raised her hand. "No, I'm not crazy, if that's what you're about to say. I just think you might have overreacted to seeing Charlotte's name. She might have just wanted to say hello to Gabe. You're just fixated on the worst-case scenario because *you have feelings for him*. And you had a bad experience with Colin."

Angel waited until Bernadette finished talking. Her voice was gentle, not pushy, and hearing her say the words made them even more real.

Yes, she *did* have feelings for Gabe. Feelings that had resurrected from the time she was sixteen and had become exponentially stronger. And she didn't know what to do with them.

"He won't bite if you go over and be up front with him, Angel."

"And what exactly would I say?" She frowned, drumming her fingers on the island countertop.

"That you shouldn't have left so quickly last night, and that you'd like to talk. *Easy-peasy*. And then you apologize, he looks at you with his luminous blue-green eyes and holds out his hand. You take it and he pulls you gently into his arms, and—"

"Stop, Bernie!" Angel put her hands on her hips. "You are such a dreamer."

"Okay, maybe I am. But maybe you should start dreaming about possibilities, Angel. I see the way Gabe looks at you. Trust me, I haven't seen him look at any other woman that way. And believe me, a lot of women have tried to get his attention."

Angel let out a big sigh. "Okay, I'll… I'll think about it while I change."

Bernadette grinned. "I'll go find some packing boxes. We'll talk later." She strode to the front door. "And be prepared to give me details," she said, and winked back at Angel.

Angel changed into a pair of pale yellow Capri pants and a white T-shirt. As she was slipping into her running shoes, the first drops of rain tapped against the side window of the front door. Unperturbed, she grabbed one of Gramsy's umbrellas from the corner bin and her light all-weather jacket. *You have to make peace with the weather if you're a true Maritimer*, Gramsy told Angel during her visits. *You can't let a few raindrops stop you.* And they would work in the garden together, or walk the beach, or walk to a neighbor's for afternoon tea. Angel would always enjoy their outings, and sometimes Bernadette would join them. *And Gabe, too.*

Angel took a deep breath. Could Bernadette be right about Charlotte? And that Angel was creating unnecessary drama around seeing her name pop up on a call to Gabe? She supposed it *was* possible.

Suddenly she felt foolish. Her imagination had gone wild, and if Bernadette could see that she had feelings for Gabe, maybe Gabe had seen that also. Her heart began a quiet drumming. Was Gabe thinking about possibilities? Could *she* start dreaming about possibilities between them, too?

Any aspirations she'd had about Colin had disintegrated after his deception, and after that, she hadn't allowed herself to get close enough to anyone to allow dreams to nudge into her thoughts during the day or night.

Now, remembering how close she and Gabe had gotten on the beach and then under the stars sent a current of heat spiraling through her. She was grateful for the intermittent breeze that cooled her cheeks.

Doing some deep breathing, Angel started briskly toward the road that would take her to Gabe's, rather than the path to the beach. She gazed at the flower garden that ran across the B&B and the window boxes and the pots on the front steps, and her heart ached at the beauty Gramsy had created. The bursts of color reminded her of some of the paintings of Nova Scotia's Maud Lewis, who had left a legacy of her brilliant works, created in her tiny decorated house that now held a celebrated spot in the Halifax art gallery.

Flowers always uplifted Angel, and as she walked, she told herself to stay positive and to keep an open mind—and heart—about possibilities. The future wasn't clear to her, and she found that a little scary, given her penchant for having things under control—*her control*. But maybe she should let go a little and allow the universe to guide her, instead of *her* taking the reins all the time.

As she neared the estate, Angel felt a gust of wind swirl around her and her umbrella turned inside out. She tried to fix it but one of the spokes broke off. The gentle sprinkling of rain that had accompanied her this far quickly changed to a shower. Giving up on the umbrella, she made a run for Gabe's front door. By the time she reached it, her clothes were partially soaked and the rain was running down her hair in streams. Ordinarily, Angel would have been annoyed or distressed, but to her surprise, she felt neither emotion. She set down the broken umbrella and rang the doorbell. She was squeezing the excess water out of her hair when the door opened.

Gabe's eyes widened and then skimmed over her. He was wearing a bathrobe and slippers, and Angel felt embarrassed that she had caught him in this state.

"Is it my cab, Gabe?"

The voice preceded the woman, who, unlike Gabe, was fully dressed. Her red hair was long and silky, and her eyes were a startling green, matching her sleeveless sundress. Angel's heart plummeted. This had to be Charlotte.

As much as Angel wanted to run away, her shoes felt leaden. She stood under the front-door awning, and from the once-over Charlotte was now giving her, Angel could only imagine the picture she made.

Gabe glanced from Charlotte to her. "Angel—"

"Sorry, I should have called first. I just wanted to discuss the meeting with the lawyer," she lied, avoiding his gaze. At that moment, a cab turned into the driveway.

"I better grab my handbag," Charlotte said, and rushed inside.

Angel wasted no time in turning away. The cab slowed to a stop and Angel ran past it.

"Angel, wait, *please*."

Gabe's voice was urgent, but she ignored it, quickening her pace. Why had she let Bernadette convince her to go over to his place? What a complete and utter fool she was to have believed that she meant something to him.

She cringed at the thought of Gabe in his robe and the fact that Charlotte had spent the night with him. Her jaw clenched. *Fool me once, shame on him. Fool me twice, shame on me.* She wanted to scream and let out her sadness, anger, disappointment and regret.

By the time she reached Gramsy's, she was out of breath and completely drenched, but she didn't go inside. She needed to walk out her disillusionment and frustration. The same horrible feelings she had experienced when she had found out that Colin was married.

Angel took the path down to the beach, and headed in the direction away from Gabe's place.

Now she was convinced there was no place for her on the island. No reason for her to ever reconsider a move. Absolutely no reason at all.

* * *

Gabe went upstairs to his room to change as soon as Charlotte left. It was unfortunate that Angel arrived at the moment she did, with him in his robe and Charlotte at his place. What she didn't know was that he was unaware that his ex-fiancée would show up uninvited. Charlotte explained that when she found out that Ross knew Gabe, she asked him for Gabe's address, saying that they were friends from the past and she had misplaced his contact information.

Ross innocently gave her the information and she arranged for a cab. When she arrived, she invited herself in and sauntered into the living room, claiming that she needed to talk to Gabe before she made her next move.

"I need to know if there's a chance for us, Gabe," she had stated bluntly after Angel left. "My business here ends in a couple of days, and then I have a week to myself. I am not going to stick around and waste my time if you're not interested."

You had a hard time sticking around in the past, Gabe wanted to say. He was silent for a few moments, choosing his words carefully. "Charlotte, I don't think small-town living on Cape Breton Island is the kind of lifestyle you want or need."

"I could fly back and forth to Scotland when I get bored," she said with a smile. "Like you do."

"Charlotte, I don't return to Scotland because I'm bored. I don't get bored here. I love this island and I love my life here."

She tossed back her hair and her green eyes narrowed. "Have you found someone? Is that why you're not interested?"

"Charlotte, even if I hadn't found someone, I wouldn't be interested."

She frowned.

"I'm not trying to be mean. It's just that our priorities are different. *We're* different. You deserve someone who wants the same things you do."

Her eyes widened. "Is it that woman who showed up like a bedraggled kitten on your doorstep?"

Gabe had to control his mouth. "Your cab is waiting," he said curtly. "And that woman has more heart in her little finger than most people." *Than you*, he wanted to add, but he didn't want to stoop to her level. He stared at her pointedly. "And yes, I love her and want to spend the rest of my life with her." *Even if she doesn't know it yet.*

Charlotte's sculpted eyebrows went up and her mouth dropped open. "Well, that settles that, then," she said, with a curt laugh. She turned to open the door. "Have a nice life, Gabe."

"I will," he said. "Thanks."

She gave him a look of resignation and let herself out. He wasted no time in going upstairs to change. He felt breathless as he dressed in a pair of jeans and hoodie. Breathless for voicing what he had, up to now, kept in his heart...that he loved Angel. Acknowledging it openly made him feel exhilarated, but he knew that at the moment, Angel was feeling anything but.

He had to go after her and make her understand that Charlotte had no place in his life, and that *she* was the one he wanted. He took the stairs two at a time and grabbed his all-weather jacket from the hall tree.

He drove to the B&B and rang the doorbell and, moments later, opened the door slightly and called out Angel's name. If she was out, she couldn't have gone far. He took a chance that she might be on the beach. He ran down the path and couldn't see anyone on his side of the beach, but he spotted a figure in the opposite direction. The rain and the ocean spray from the increasing winds blurred his vision so he couldn't be sure if it was Angel, but he was willing to take the chance.

He broke into a run. The wind kept whipping his hood off and he stopped trying to keep it on. The sound of the waves surging and cresting filled his ears. He could barely hear his own thoughts as he tried to formulate his words to Angel.

The figure was closer. He squeezed his eyes shut and then shielded them with his hands to have a better look. It *was* Angel. He felt his heart begin its drumming. "Angel!" he called out, but a cramp in his leg made him falter, and he felt himself collapsing on the beach as an intense pain gripped his calf. *"Damn!"* Gabe started to massage the area, but cringed at the pain. When he thought he wouldn't be able to endure it any longer, it suddenly subsided.

Gabe continued to rub the area, reluctant to stand up right away and risk getting another cramp.

"I suppose I should offer you a hand to get up…before you're washed out to sea."

Gabe twisted his head so sharply that he felt a burn along a nerve in his neck. "Angel!" he said, his voice cracking. He stared up at her, with the rain streaming down her face and hair, and unconcerned about her drenched clothes. *An island girl.*

CHAPTER TWENTY-TWO

WHEN ANGEL HAD heard Gabe call, her first instinct was to ignore him and keep walking. But when she turned and saw him landing on the beach, her heart had jolted, thinking he was hurt and remembering how he had helped her when she'd injured her calf. Now she saw the look of relief in his eyes.

"Leg cramp," he said huskily. "I'm okay now. But thanks for offering to help." He ventured a smile. "I'll still accept a hand."

She hesitated momentarily and then extended her left hand. He pushed himself up and stood facing her without letting go of her hand. "Angel—"

"You don't need to explain, Gabe. I get the picture." She pulled her hand away but her gaze locked with his. "But I don't appreciate you taking advantage of the circumstances to lead me on." She bit her lip, recalling the swirl of desire his kisses had ignited. "It was dishonest, deceitful and just *wrong*, given the fact that you and your ex-fiancée are back together." She frowned. "I have no use for that kind of behavior. Or anyone who acts like that." Now that she had the chance, she wasn't going to keep her feelings to herself. She would let him have it. "Gramsy always spoke so highly of you. I guess she wasn't aware of this side of your personality," she said bitingly.

She paused, the rain mingling with the tears that were edging out. The waves breaking on the shore seemed to be extraordinarily loud. Usually, she loved the sound, but now, the cacophony just seemed to intensify the ache in her heart.

Gabe was looking at her intently but not making any attempt to reply. She smirked. Of course he had nothing to say. He knew she was right.

"It's too bad Gramsy wanted me to sell the B&B to you if I decided not to keep it," she continued, wanting to hurt him with her words, the way his actions had hurt her. "Under the right circumstances, I'd keep it myself and not sell it at all." She gave a bitter laugh. "But you can congratulate yourself for inching your way into Gramsy's heart," she said, her voice breaking. *And mine.* "I'll be packing up some of the items I want and leaving right after the reception in her memory. Oh, and you don't have to worry about doing any of the cooking or baking. I'll talk to Bernadette about ordering the food from Making Waves."

"Angel, stop. *Please.*"

She blinked at him, taken aback by the hurt in his eyes, and not feeling at all triumphant about it. He was as drenched as she was, and the rain had begun to intensify. He glanced beyond her shoulder and then back at her.

"Angel, please give me a chance to explain. I promise, you won't regret it. But standing here is ridiculous. The fairy hole is up ahead. At least it'll be dry."

Angel knew Gabe was talking about one of the sea caves in the area, a place that had held wonder for her as a child. Gramsy had taken her there and they'd had a picnic inside the cave, while watching the surf come roaring and crashing on the shore.

The fairy hole, tied to the sacred Mi'kmaq culture on the island, was also a place where she, Bernadette and Gabe had ventured one summer while the adults were enjoying the garden party at Gabe's parents' place.

They didn't stay long, as the deep, dark recesses of the cave had frightened Angel, being the youngest. She imagined bats, trolls and even spooky fairies lurking in the depths. They hurried back and were met with stern looks and even sterner consequences for breaking the rules and wandering off. Gabe, being the oldest, was held responsible and was grounded.

But now the cave seemed a welcome respite.

She nodded curtly and they both ran for it. A couple of minutes later, they were standing just inside. Angel glanced warily at the ceiling. There was no sign of bats at this time of day, thank goodness.

She caught Gabe's gaze and the amusement in his eyes, and she suspected he was recalling the incident when they were young.

"At least now I won't get grounded when we return," he said huskily.

"You should be grounded anyway," she said curtly.

"Touché," he said, and sighed. "Okay, Angel, now can I try to explain?"

She shrugged. "It doesn't matter."

"To me it does." He gazed at her intently. "Charlotte came to the island of her own accord. She did have business here and she did try to take the opportunity to see if there was a chance we could get back together. I made it clear that I wasn't interested."

"In your robe?" Angel's words slipped out.

Gabe's brows lifted and she knew that he'd guessed her implication.

"I wasn't expecting her to come to my place. In fact, I had never given her my address. She got it from Ross, saying that she lost my contact information. She came over this morning. I had just taken a shower and when I heard the doorbell, I thought it was *you*. I didn't want to go and get changed and risk you not being there when I opened the door."

Angel blinked, her mind trying to process his every word. Could she believe him?

"Angel, I was finished with Charlotte three years ago. Yes, I was hurt when she broke off with me, but it didn't take me long to realize that we weren't right for each other. Look, she came to Mara's yesterday. She apologized for not being there for me when my parents died and she hoped we could reconcile. I accepted her apology. And... I thought you had no interest in seeing if there was a possibility that we could—"

"So you let her believe that there was a chance for a reconciliation?" Angel forced herself to ask the question.

"I said nothing, which I regret. Which is why she made a second attempt to push the issue. Just before you arrived on my doorstep." He smiled. "Looking like a beautiful, lost, drenched kitten that I wanted to rescue." He reached for her hand and squeezed it gently. "You bolted, and I wanted to run after you, but I had to change. *After* making it very clear to Charlotte that she was barking up the wrong tree." He took her other hand and gazed into her eyes. "I told her I loved you," he said softly. "But I should have told you that *first*."

Angel felt her eyes prickling. He loved her.

And the leap of her heart confirmed what she knew deep down—that she loved him too. She blinked, wanting to believe him fully, but there was something she had to get out. "My boyfriend cheated on me, made me believe I was the only one in his life. Turns out he was married," she said. "I told him I never wanted to see him again." She looked at Gabe through blurred vision. "I could never be with a man I couldn't trust."

"And you thought I was taking advantage of you while I was involved with Charlotte." He nodded. "I get it. And I swear, Angel, as Gramsy is my witness up above, that you can trust me." He drew his arms around her. "I wouldn't risk lying and having Gramsy haunt me for the rest of my life." His chin grazed her cheek. "A life I want to spend with *you*," he murmured gently. "If you'll have me."

Angel shifted to meet his gaze, the dark green depths of his eyes mirroring the turbulent gulf waters. She felt a tremor go through her, anticipating what lay ahead for them. But could she make a permanent move to the island?

Gabe brought her hands to his lips and kissed them. "I love it here, Angel… But I love you more. We drifted apart in the past, and we can't let that ever happen again. If you want to stay in Toronto, I'll make my home there with you, and we can spend our summers here. I can always check in on Mara's, like I do with Maeve's." His eyes were bright as they pierced into hers. "You are my home, Angel."

Angel felt her heart do a flip at what Gabe was willing to give up for her. Her mind flipped, too. Relocating to Chéticamp wasn't as impossible as it had first seemed. So what if she lost her seniority? She could still teach with the same salary rate.

She had so much to gain here. And even if she didn't get a teaching job right away, she'd be happy getting reacquainted with the place that had enchanted her throughout the years, giving her memories to cherish. Only now, she could make new memories with the man she loved. Her Scottish Cape Bretoner.

Angel lifted her hand to tenderly touch his cheek. "The island has always been a part of my heart. But with you here, my heart is now full. I'm here to stay, Gabe." As her eyes began to prickle, she imagined Longfellow's Evangeline must have felt the same way when she was reunited with her Gabriel. She said as much toGabe and was startled to see his beautiful eyes misting.

"Only our story together will last a long, long time," he said huskily. "We found each other after again after ten years. No more searching. I love you, Evangeline. *My angel.*"

"I love you, Gabriel," she murmured, stroking

his jaw. She reached into her pocket and fished out the pink heart shell and chain she had retrieved from her bedroom closet before heading to his place.

Gabe looked at it in wonder before placing it around her neck. He bent to kiss her. She wrapped her arms around his neck and allowed herself to reciprocate his passion, the rush of the waves and the salty breeze stirring her soul. She was exactly where she was meant to be, she thought, catching her breath to meet his gaze. On Chéticamp Island.

And in Gabe's eyes and heart!

* * * * *

If you enjoyed this story, check out these other great reads from Rosanna Battigelli

Falling for the Sardinian Baron
Rescued by the Guarded Tycoon
Caribbean Escape with the Tycoon
Captivated by Her Italian Boss

All available now!

Get up to 4 Free Books!

We'll send you 2 free books from each series you try PLUS a free Mystery Gift.

FREE Value Over $25

Both the **Harlequin® Historical** and **Harlequin® Romance** series feature compelling novels filled with emotion and simmering romance.

YES! Please send me 2 FREE novels from the Harlequin Historical or Harlequin Romance series and my FREE Mystery Gift (gift is worth about $10 retail). After receiving them, if I don't wish to receive any more books, I can return the shipping statement marked "cancel." If I don't cancel, I will receive 5 brand-new Harlequin Historical books every month and be billed just $6.39 each in the U.S. or $7.19 each in Canada, or 4 brand-new Harlequin Romance Larger-Print books every month and be billed just $7.19 each in the U.S. or $7.99 each in Canada, a savings of 20% off the cover price. It's quite a bargain! Shipping and handling is just 50¢ per book in the U.S. and $1.25 per book in Canada.* I understand that accepting the 2 free books and gift places me under no obligation to buy anything. I can always return a shipment and cancel at any time by calling the number below. The free books and gift are mine to keep no matter what I decide.

Choose one: ☐ **Harlequin Historical** (246/349 BPA G36Y)   ☐ **Harlequin Romance Larger-Print** (119/319 BPA G36Y)   ☐ **Or Try Both!** (246/349 & 119/319 BPA G36Z)

Name (please print)

Address   Apt. #

City   State/Province   Zip/Postal Code

Email: Please check this box ☐ if you would like to receive newsletters and promotional emails from Harlequin Enterprises ULC and its affiliates. You can unsubscribe anytime.

Mail to the Harlequin Reader Service:
IN U.S.A.: P.O. Box 1341, Buffalo, NY 14240-8531
IN CANADA: P.O. Box 603, Fort Erie, Ontario L2A 5X3

Want to explore our other series or interested in ebooks? Visit www.ReaderService.com or call 1-800-873-8635.

---

*Terms and prices subject to change without notice. Prices do not include sales taxes, which will be charged (if applicable) based on your state or country of residence. Canadian residents will be charged applicable taxes. Offer not valid in Quebec. This offer is limited to one order per household. Books received may not be as shown. Not valid for current subscribers to the Harlequin Historical or Harlequin Romance series. All orders subject to approval. Credit or debit balances in a customer's account(s) may be offset by any other outstanding balance owed by or to the customer. Please allow 4 to 6 weeks for delivery. Offer available while quantities last.

Your Privacy—Your information is being collected by Harlequin Enterprises ULC, operating as Harlequin Reader Service. For a complete summary of the information we collect, how we use this information and to whom it is disclosed, please visit our privacy notice located at https://corporate.harlequin.com/privacy-notice. Notice to California Residents – Under California law, you have specific rights to control and access your data. For more information on these rights and how to exercise them, visit https://corporate.harlequin.com/california-privacy. For additional information for residents of other U.S. states that provide their residents with certain rights with respect to personal data, visit https://corporate.harlequin.com/other-state-residents-privacy-rights/.

HHHRLP25